BOOKS BY TIM MCBAIN & L.T. VARGUS

Casting Shadows Everywhere
Fade to Black (Awake in the Dark #1)
Bled White (Awake in the Dark #2)

BLED WHITE

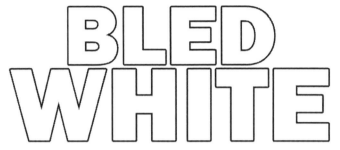

BLED WHITE

TIM MCBAIN & L.T. VARGUS

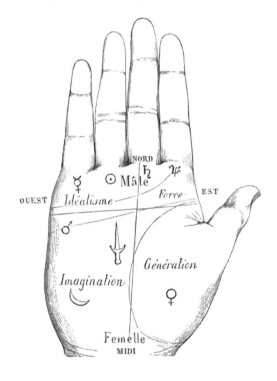

SMARMY PRESS

BLED WHITE

- 1 -

My consciousness returns and lifts me out of the dark. It feels like I'm rising to the surface of the ocean, floating up and up into the light.

I find myself back in the cell, but it's all different. The walls are pale around me like sickly skin never touched by the sun. It's not just the walls, though. The floor, the bars, the blanket, the ceiling: everything is bled white like the life has been sucked out while I was away. I rub my eyes, but the drained look remains.

And then I notice that my hand is also washed out. My skin sheens opaque white. Texturally it's similar to maggot flesh. Actually, the paleness makes everything look a little bulbous and insect like. I think this is an optical illusion. They say that maggot flesh adds ten pounds.

My hand looks so dead that I wiggle it just to make sure everything still works. My fingers writhe like white worms.

Somehow none of this alarms me. In fact, as I do maggoty jazz hands again, it occurs to me that I'm laughing.

"What's so funny?" a voice says from the hall. The sound echoes and seems far away, but I know it must be close.

I try to sit up.

Fail.

I teeter my head forward, and though my neck feels about

as sturdy as a rubber band, it holds me up long enough to see.

It's Babinaux, picking through keys on a big key ring. She looks all pale as well, though maybe less maggoty than me - must be her bone structure. I forgot that she was here to rescue me.

Pretty sweet.

I wonder if there will be food soon.

I let my rubber band neck snap back, and my head flops onto the cot, bouncing a couple of times, which feels more pleasant than it probably sounds. It's like a trampoline for the brain. I lift my head and let it go a couple more times, my cerebrum rattling against my skull in a nice way. Every time my head lands, it feels like fingers massage the place where my shoulders meet the neck.

"Are you OK?" she says.

"Good," I say. "Good stuff."

"Well then, let's go," she says. "We might not have a lot of time."

Glancing in her direction, I realize the cell door is open and she's standing half in my area. Her posture suggests impatience, like she has been there for a while already.

"Oh," I say. "Sorry."

Not sure what the big rush is. I consider explaining the brain trampoline and decide against it.

I stand up, wobble a moment, and take a step forward. The ground feels squishy underfoot like I'm walking on a layer of marshmallow. I take long, exaggerated steps like that will somehow help me keep my balance. It's hard to feel secure when you're walking on fluff like this.

I shimmy out of the cell and Ms. Babinaux takes my arm to

help steady me.

"Are you sure you're alright?" she says, her lips two flaps of faded meat.

"It's all good," I say. "A little squishier than I might like, but…"

We move through the door into a hallway. The cinder block walls remind me of a college dorm. It's hard to say what all of this might look like without the color being sucked out of everything.

"What is this place?" I say.

"It's an old hospital," she says. "The League bought it years ago. The plan was to rehab it, but the progress has been slow."

I really want to run my hand against the wall, to feel the cool of the painted concrete on my fingertips. But Ms. Babinaux has my arm in a death grip, and she's moving with some urgency, dragging me along like a puppy that wants to stop and smell everything.

I bet there's food wherever we're going. I wonder what it could be. It strikes me that I'm neither hungry nor full. It just seems like food would be pleasant. I like the way it tastes.

Wait. We're in a darker hallway now with smooth concrete walls. It stretches out into the distance so far that I can't see the end, at least not clearly. I think we went downstairs at some point, which would be weird since we were already in the basement.

I kind of want to say "What demonry is this?" but I opt for: "Where are we?"

"I told you. These are the tunnels under the hospital," she says. "There's a back way out. This way we know we won't run into anybody."

We're quiet for a moment. The only sound is our feet squishing into the marshmallow foam.

"Did they drug you?" she says.

This is a good question. I do feel like I'm walking around in a dream, though I believe it to be real. I try to remember how this all came about, but it feels like some of that stuff was weeks ago. I remember… um…

White. The white is important.

And then the image bursts into my head: beams of white light flaring in all directions. I lie in the alley. My alley. And someone else was there before that. Before the white, I mean. The hooded man. I killed him, but then it wasn't him. It was like a dream where the shapes shift and the scenery changes and the people all change into someone else. The hooded man turned into Amity.

Or wait. Maybe it was always Amity. Glenn's daughter wore the hood the whole time.

Yeah. Yeah, that's right.

Well, that's a little upsetting.

OK, wait again. What did Babinaux just say? Was it something about food?

"Jeffrey," she says. "Did they drug you?"

Damn it. Not food.

She stares at me. Her eyes look like she has milky contacts in.

"I don't think so," I say. "I had a seizure when you left the room. And now everything is bled white."

"Bled white?" she says.

I nod.

"All the life and color got sucked right out," I say. "I feel a

4

little effed up, too, I guess. Hard to remember all the moving pieces."

She presses her lips together, and they look like mating albino caterpillars. It strikes me that the tip of my nose is freezing cold.

The end of the previously endless hall takes shape in front of us. There's a stairway.

"Where are we going?" I say.

"I'm taking you home," she says.

"Won't people just try to abduct me again?" I say.

"I'll have a couple of guys keep an eye on the place," she says.

We climb the staircase and it leads to a steel door. Babinaux opens it, and a rectangle of sunlight glares in the doorway. I squint as we cross the threshold, taking in a grass field that gives way to an empty parking lot in the distance. Turning around, we walked out of what looks like a brick storage shed. You'd probably never guess that it leads down into a weird underground lair if you walked past it.

"Our ride should be here momentarily," she says.

I glance over her shoulder and see the moon in the sky behind her. Even though it's probably mid-morning, the moon is out. Seems weird in a way, but then I guess the moon is always out when Babinaux is around somehow.

- 2 -

By the time the Lincoln pulls into Glenn's driveway, I can make out a red hue to the front door. I swivel my head around, and everywhere I look, the color begins to seep back into things, the white fading away. It's slow, but if I watch it closely enough I can see some progress. It reminds me of something that would happen in a cartoon.

I get out of the car, and my feet don't really squish into the sidewalk as I move toward the front door, at least not like before. It's more like walking on a thick layer of hardboiled egg whites than marshmallow now. It still gives under my weight but in a different way and not as much.

I realize that my state of euphoria is also wearing off. I still feel pleasant, but as I drift back toward normal, I understand how "high" I really was before, for lack of a better term. At the time, I didn't grasp that.

I hesitate outside the door. For some reason, I know Glenn won't be here. The Explorer still sits in the driveway, but I have this sense that when he said he'd try to come back for me, he didn't mean he'd try to come back to the jail cell to get me. He meant it in a bigger way than that.

As I set foot in the doorway, I'm greeted by the mess. Pictures and glass shards and utensils and couch stuffing crowd the floor. I forgot about all of that until I swung the door open.

Yep. The place remains trashed, and these cats didn't lift so much as a paw to do anything about it. Figures.

Against my better judgment, I decide to feed the beasts anyway. The second I lift a can from the stack, Mardy trots into the kitchen. When I pop the lid off, the rest of the pack prowls onto the scene.

Leroy scarfs his food and then tries to steal everybody else's meat, so I have to stand guard until they're all done. Turns out watching cats eat is not super entertaining.

With that out of the way, I get down to business. I rifle through the fridge and take a peek into the cabinets. I even skim through the cans and boxes of food strewn across the floor. There are many viable options here – smoked turkey and honey glazed ham in the form of an expensive brand of lunch meat that I've never tried, Glenn's homemade pickles, a variety of Oreos, some strawberry pop tarts, and an embarrassment of soft drinks.

After much deliberation, I decide to have a glass of orange juice and a blueberry Nutri-grain bar. I realize this is an odd combination, the kind of sweet upon sweet menu building often exhibited by a toddler. Maybe I'm vitamin C deprived or something, but it sounds great to me.

I have big plans to clear a spot on the couch, sit down and really savor this food and drink, but I can't wait. I sip the orange juice as soon as I pour it. I feel the cool fluid wash over my tongue, the acidity tingling on my palate, and then separate waves of sweet and tart hitting at the same time. I guess my senses must be heightened like crazy, because the only way I can describe the flavor is profound. In fact, it is beyond a flavor. It's an experience.

Overwhelmed, I set the glass down on the counter and close my eyes. Time passes. I feel like I can hear the ocean lapping against a beach in the distance. When I open my eyes, it feels like I've gone somewhere else and back again.

I gather my wits along with my drink and breakfast bar and head to the sofa. I scoot piles of couch innards to the left and right and plop down in the middle.

I peel open the foil wrapping on the Nutri-grain bar, the crinkle only adding to the anticipation. I examine it. The bottom looks quite fake, really – the browning and dimpled spots a little too even, too perfect. The smell wafts at me aggressively, all fruit and sweet in my face. My mouth waters.

This is getting pretty intense in a hurry.

I rewrap the bar and set it down on the coffee table, taking a deep breath as I do so. I tell myself to relax. We just got to the pool, Grobnagger. No need to go straight for the damn high dive. Let's wade in and get used to the water first.

I take another sip of juice, and it happens again – the tingle, the waves, my eyes snapping shut involuntarily. I set the glass down and take another deep breath.

As I exhale, I try to relax all of the muscles in my neck and back. It feels like the best massage I've ever had. I slowly lean forward, my eyes droop closed and a calm comes over me. The whole universe is still. I hear that sound again that I know isn't really there, like waves rolling in and out. Within about 10 seconds, I'm asleep.

I start awake a few seconds later, saliva oozing out of the corner of my mouth.

I can't remember ever falling asleep so quickly. I'm usually the guy that rolls around for 45 minutes every night no matter what, but this eating thing is turning out to be kind of exhausting, I guess.

I look over the faintly purple foil wrapper and glass nearly full of pale orange liquid on the table in front of me. They're enticing, but not yet. It's too much. I need to ease into this. I'll just sit for a second, and then I'll eat. Just a second.

A hope wells in me for no good reason that I can think of. It's like a buoy that won't sink no matter how many waves of bad things wash over it.

With my eyes closed, bits of the prior evening come back to me in flashes – the shattered cup, Glenn's speech and exit through the concrete wall, my encounter with Amity in the alley and the white light everywhere. Even as it all comes back to me, I still only feel hope and empathy and a new understanding. Because I know if I get the chance, I will make things right with Louise and see where things might go between us. And something about that makes it feel like everything else will work out fine.

My head tilts forward again, and I'm asleep.

A bell chimes, and I shake myself awake in time to hear the tail end of the sound. The mess of Glenn's living room surrounds me again. I lift my hand to my face, and a swath of couch stuffing clings to my fingers. Sweat beads on the orange juice glass, and the untouched Nutri-grain bar sits next to it. I press my fingertips to the glass and find it's still cool.

Thinking back, though I was asleep, I know the bell chimed at least twice before the one that woke me. I remember hearing it in my dream.

The only clock in the room is smashed, so I have little sense of how long I was out beyond the temp of the juice. More importantly, perhaps: What the eff could the tolling bell have been? I could still hear it trailing off when I woke, so I'm pretty sure it wasn't just a dream.

On cue, it chimes again, and I gaze up at the ceiling as it seems to be coming from up high. From above? Is this another metaphysical test of some kind? A bell is a little ominous, though, right? I mean, for whom does this fucker toll?

There's the clatter of something solid striking metal. It's a familiar noise, but it takes a moment to register. Someone's knocking at the door. I guess that makes the chime a doorbell.

Some genius I turned out to be.

I hustle to the door, wading through the junk pile, and peek through the peep hole. It's her. Her face looks all flushed.

I open the door, and Louise stands before me. The sunlight glints down onto her. It's so much brighter on that side of the doorway. The shade shrouds my side in black. Her face twists into a scowl as she makes eye contact. Her complexion has been splotched with pink before but never looked so uniformly rosy as it does now, and that's with the world still faded a little white for me.

"Hi," I say.

"Listen," she says. "I get it. You're the closed off type, the loner, the outsider, whatever you want to call it. Fine. I understand this premise, alright, but I don't accept it."

"What?" I say.

"I'm not going to let you push me away, Jeffrey," she says. "I know that's how you operate. You push everyone away. You withdraw out of fear, and I won't allow it. I think that we both know-"

Before she can finish her sentence, I lean through the doorway, my face drenched in daylight, and kiss her. The last thing I see before I close my eyes is her eyes going wide and her expression softening.

And then I wonder if my breath tastes like orange juice. I guess there are worse things.

Undaunted by this breathy query, I slide my hands around her waist and pull her close to me, through the doorway and into the shade.

I explain the events of the prior evening as I clear off another spot on the couch and we sit.

"You didn't have to go to all the trouble of cleaning the place just for little ole me," she says as she kicks pieces of a shattered ceramic coaster out from under her seating area.

"Yeah, sorry about this," I say.

"I'm just playin'," she says. "It's hardly your fault a bunch of wackos trashed the place in the name of magic."

I nod. And then I take a sip of the orange juice without thinking about it. I brace myself for an overwhelming taste explosion as the beverage crosses my lips, but it's only mildly orgasmic. I guess I must make a weird face, though.

"You alright, weirdo?" Louise says, laughing.

I look over to see her staring at me out of the corners of her eyes, her head tilted away.

"Huh?" I say. "Oh."

I set the glass down.

"You make the craziest faces, you know that?" she says.

"I guess so," I say.

She opens her mouth to speak again, but a buzz and beep

emit from her purse, interrupting her. She pulls out her phone, taps and swipes the screen. Her brow furrows a moment as she reads, and then the creases unfold and a smile curves her lips.

"Want to see something crazy?" she says.

- 3 -

The charred body stretches before us, blistered and pocked with red and black. Forehead skin pools on the right side of the face, still soft from melting and oozing to gravity's whim. The tissue congeals there, covering one eye. I can hardly tell an eye socket exists underneath.

She doesn't say anything, but Louise puts a hand on my shoulder. Her other hand forms a shield in front of her mouth like she might vomit every which way in a second. I don't think this is what she envisioned when she smiled and asked me about seeing something crazy.

My eyes drift from Louise back to the body. Bone glints where flames ate away the eyelid of the other eye. The lack of flesh makes the eyeball on that side look bulbous like it's about to pop.

Dennis pokes his police baton into the corpse's ribs, and something crunches like an overcooked piece of bacon.

"Jesus Christ, dude," I say.

My feet grind into the gravel as I take a step back and avert my eyes. Dennis laughs, his fingers drumming at his beer belly in delight.

"Aw, he don't mind, Grobnagger," he says, gesturing at the body with the stick.

Louise knows Dennis from her investigations – he's one of

her contacts in the police department - so now I know Dennis as well, which is really too bad.

I look back at the corpse. A few patches of smooth scalp remain, contrasting with the rippled and bubbled swaths. Angry folds and crevices pucker the skin on the neck. My eyes keep tracing over the edge of the mouth where the blackened remnants of the lips give way to the white of the teeth.

The body sprawls in the center of a vacant lot. Judging by the chain link fence around us and some of the bigger pieces of concrete underfoot, I know the building that stood here once was razed to the ground back when the city still tended to such things. Now weeds sprout up in clusters through the chunks of cinder block. A dandelion smears its yellow on the back of my pant leg.

I'm not concerned with the plant life, however. I take a step back and draw my eyes away from the face. The burns leave few identifiable details from the waist up, but the legs suffered little damage. I point to the bottom of the maroon robe draping the ankles.

"That's a League robe?" I say.

Dennis nods.

"A genu-wine ceremonial League of Light robe," he says. "Way I heard Detective Miller sayin', they only bust these things out for initiations and such. Body wasn't burned out here, though. It was burned someplace else and dumped here. That's according to Miller as well."

His lips purse like he's about to spit on the ground, but he stops himself, perhaps remembering that this is a crime scene.

"Figured it was only a matter of time before there was a bunch of dead bodies out this way," he says, gesturing the baton at the land around us. "These damn dirt worshippers ain't but troublemakers and head cases."

Louise turns away. I can't decide where she stands on the vom-o-meter.

"Is ya'll hungry?" Dennis says.

"Uh," I say, glancing away from the crispy body. "No."

Louise shakes her head.

"Damn," Dennis says. "Cause my belly is downright angry. I didn't have no time for breakfast."

"Have the detectives interviewed any of the League people yet?" I say.

"Tried," Dennis says. "They ain't such a cooperative bunch. I guess when you're in the business of savin' souls, it don't look good when one of your people shows up deep fried and all."

We are silent for a moment.

"God, I'm hungry," Dennis says, prodding at the chest with the stick again.

"Stop playing with the goddamn thing!" Louise says, her face all dark now, her eyes open too wide like a boxer moving in for the kill shot after his opponent's knees buckle.

"Huh?" he says.

"It's a human being," she says. "Do you have to keep poking it like that?"

"Oh," he says.

"Not to mention that this is a murder scene," she says. "You're tampering with the victim's body for shit's sake. I mean, who the hell ever let you be a cop?"

Dennis sticks his lips out in a frown. He pulls the baton away from the body and twirls it, almost slapping it into his palm but stopping at the last minute. He kneels to try to wipe

15

the ashy residue off of it in the weeds.

"You know I didn't have to bring y'all out here," he says. "I don't have to give you all the info I give you, miss snippy. I do that as a kindness. For a friend."

Louise's crazy eyes shrink back to normal width. She looks poised to apologize, but Dennis stands and goes on.

"It ain't no thing, though," he says. "Listen, if you're hungry, I'm 'bout to go to Krazy Chicken for lunch once the coroner gets here. Fried chicken. Homemade slaw. Biscuits slathered with honey. It's good as hell."

Louise and I just look at each other.

"Believe it or not, staring at this cooked human body isn't exactly whetting my appetite," I say.

"Whatever, dude," Dennis says. "A man's gotta eat."

As the Passat carries us back to Glenn's house, I stare out the window, letting my eyes go out of focus so all I see is a blur smearing past on the side of the road. The distraction doesn't help. The image of the charred body flickers in my imagination, blur or no blur.

It ranks up there among the worst ways to go, I think - consumed by fire. And the idea that the same people that abducted me could be behind this murder isn't lost on me.

Without meaning to, I imagine the flames crawling over my body, searing, blistering, melting my flesh. I shudder.

"Are you cold?" Louise says, reaching to adjust the AC.

"No," I say. "It's… I'm fine."

She looks at me for a long time.

"OK," she says.

Seeing the blue of her eyes, I realize that everything looks pretty much normal again – no more milky eyeballs, no more faded meat mouths. I hold up my hand and wiggle my fingers, and they look like regular old fingers again.

I guess there's a small amount of relief to the white world thing coming to an end. On the other hand, I was never that upset about everything going maggoty, so the soothing sensation is quite mild. In a way, I think my reaction might be weirder than everything else about it. When your hand looks like a pile of worms, you're supposed to be a little upset, right? I mean, I don't know if laughing is an appropriate response there. At the time, I was pretty pleased with it all, though.

I roll my neck and then lean my head back on the headrest. My eyes drift shut of their own accord. I really should be hungry by now, but I'm not. The last thing I ate was some garbage water Thai food, which feels like it transpired about six months ago. Instead, I'm only sleepy.

I sit up to avoid slumber.

"Did any of them seem like killers to you?" I say.

"What do you mean?" she says.

"You've spent a good bit of time around the League people," I say. "Did any of them seem capable of murder?"

Her eyes point skyward as she thinks a moment, her hands stroking at the wheel of the car.

"None in particular," she says. "But my line of work makes you realize real quick that almost anyone is capable of almost anything."

I scratch the back of my neck.

"I guess that makes sense," I say.

Damn. What the hell? I get locked up in a cell and then a burned body pops up within twelve or so hours? Not great. I

Tim McBain & L.T. Vargus

wish Glenn was here. He'd know what to make of this.

The Passat glides into the driveway behind the Explorer. I take a deep breath, exhale and look over at Louise. She rubs at the bridge of her nose with thumb and index finger.

"I don't suppose you want to help me clean this mess up?" I say, doing that nonchalant shrug thing that seemed to win Glenn over with such ease.

She narrows her eyes at me.

"I guess," she says.

- 4 -

First, we clear the biggest objects from the living room floor. The shattered bits get thrown out, and the pictures with broken frames get shoved in a closet for Glenn to deal with later. Within a few minutes, we've already made a big difference. With the fallen pictures and broken glass out of way and toppled plants set right, it begins to look like a livable room again.

Then we split up. Louise shoves the stuffing back into the couch cushions and sews them up. I figure we can throw a slipcover over it later and no one will know the difference.

While she does that, I dust bust the areas where soil got ground into the carpet when the plants went down. Once the dirt spots fade away, I broaden my range of attack to sweep up the random debris strewn about the rest of the room. The vacuum keeps finding loads of filth even after the floor passes the eyeball test, and I have to empty Glenn's Dirt Devil three times before I'm through.

After just over an hour, the living room looks to be in order. This is good. Now we just have to do every other room in the house.

I pick up dishes and utensils off of the kitchen floor and throw them in the sink. Louise checks her phone a few times and writes a couple of texts in between picking up various cans and boxes of food from the floor and shoving them back in the cupboard. I think about asking her what the messages are about, but I decide against it.

Once the floor is clear, I start loading the dishwasher, which I will need to run four times to get everything clean. As the first load runs, I move to the dining room to start the process yet again, removing fragments, remnants and scraps on the first sweep.

When I walk by the kitchen again, I see that Louise has butter melting in a frying pan.

"What's this?" I say.

"It's getting late," she says. "We need to eat."

I consider the notion.

"I'm not hungry," I say.

"Me neither," she says. "But I've solved that problem. I'm making something that tastes great whether you're hungry or not."

I nod and get back to work, taking the dust buster to task in the dining area. The Dirt Devil ruffles the fabric of the rug as it passes, spiking it up when I push forward and smoothing it down when I pull it back.

Just as I finish vacuuming, Louise enters the room with two plates each holding one and a half grilled cheese sandwiches.

I wash my hands and sit down at the dining room table that looks like a single slice taken out of a massive tree and glazed with something. In all of my time at Glenn's, this is the first time I've sat at this fancy table under the chandelier. It feels a bit silly, to be honest.

We eat, and she was right about the grilled cheese. It's good.

After the sandwiches, Louise heads home to shower and sleep, and I plan to do the same. I head for the bathroom. And after a glance in the mirror, I dig around in the cabinets until I find an electric razor.

I have this hair that sprouts on the back of my neck and the very top of my back. This is one of the many joys of getting older, I suppose, though I might be partially to blame. Years ago I shaved my head with a razor for a few months, and I shaved this peach fuzz on my neck during that time. Well, it grew back thicker as time went on. I know some people think that that's just a fallacy, that shaving doesn't affect follicles or make hair any thicker. Based on the chia pet thriving between my shoulder blades, I'm pretty sure those people are wrong.

Even worse, it's incongruous. I'm not very hairy elsewhere. I'm not your Robin Williams type. My arms and legs have light, non-offensive hair. This stuff on my neck looks slightly thicker than the stuff that hangs down in a yak's eyes.

Anyway, like I said, now it grows out, this carpet of dark fluff, and I feel like a disgusting troll. Eventually I can't take it anymore, and I go at it with an electric shaver. It's insane how much better I feel after I trim it. The loathsome feeling dies down, and I feel clean. I mean, I feel like a troll still but not a particularly disgusting one.

So I shave and shower, and my skin feels all fresh. The troll meter goes down a little more.

Once I get cleaned up, though, I find myself sitting in the living room doing nothing instead of going to bed. I sip at a tiny glass of orange juice. The flavor doesn't overpower me the way it did earlier, but it seems too acidic to be that enjoyable now, almost bitter. Even so, it's the only food item I find myself drawn to.

I flip through the channels on TV. I stare at the screen, but I can't seem to register the images flashing there nor can I hear what's being said. I imagine this is maybe what it's like for a dog to watch television. Their eyes lock onto the moving pictures, but it means nothing to them most of the time.

Through the window, I see two beams of light slice through the night and swing into the driveway. Headlights. Ah, yes. Babinaux is about due to show up for one of our night meetings, I suppose. The moon is like her bat signal or something.

I head out to meet her in the back of the Lincoln as usual.

"I assume you heard about the body from your investigator friend," she says as I climb into the vehicle.

"Yeah," I say. "I actually saw it, which was… unpleasant."

"I'd think so," she says. "Well, I have some information that your friend wouldn't have. At least not yet. That's why I'm here tonight."

"What's that?" I say.

"It's Farber," she says. "The corpse. It's Riston Farber."

"The spoon man? The one that's trying to kill me?" I say.

"That's the one," she says. "It's a big shock to our community. He had very devoted followers, and they're devastated as you'd expect."

"Who'd want to kill him?" I say.

I actually have an idea on this one, but I'm damn sure not telling her.

"It's hard to say," she says. "His two disciples, Seth Cromwell and Stan Woods, are jockeying to take his place now, and the support seems pretty split. They'd have the most to gain, so it stands to reason that one of them might have done it."

"Crazy," I say.

"The good news for you is that one of them is a moderate," she says.

I assume she's about to elaborate, but when she doesn't I'm forced to ask the obvious question:

"What the hell does the mean?" I say.

"Sorry," she says. "It's been a long day. When Farber kidnapped you and your friend, he was essentially splitting from the League. He had already started the process of making his followers believe he was becoming divine – 'forming,' he called it. I guess he felt you played some role in that."

I nod.

"One of his disciples, Stan Woods, apparently wants no part of that plan," she says. "He wants their group to rejoin the League and let you be. He's a pretty nice guy, Stan."

"I see," I say. "Well, I can get behind that plan, anyway."

She smiles.

"What about the other guy?" I say. "Does he still want to give me the old-"

I pantomime hands closing around my wind pipe.

"I'm not sure," she says, her smile fading. "I don't know him as well, but Cromwell has quite a reputation. There are a lot of stories - nasty stories - but it's hard to say which might be true. I guess I'll say that many in the League fear him. That much I know for a fact."

She scratches her nose before she goes on.

"I think his priority will be the struggle for power at the moment, though, so you're probably safe for now. And I'll still have a couple of men keeping an eye on you."

"I can respect that," I say.

She talks a bit more, but my mind starts to tune out like a dog watching TV again. Because all I can think about is the gut feeling I had when she told me Farber was dead – that Glenn was the one who killed him.

A mix of feelings tumbles inside of me like a load of delicates in the dryer, equal parts alleviation and repulsion and dread. I'm relieved that Farber isn't out there trying to kill me at the moment. For the first time since he walked through the wall, though, I'm worried about Glenn. What might he have gotten himself into? Even if he didn't kill Farber, where the hell is he? I never really felt like he could be in danger, but now it somehow seems more likely than not.

As I start the slow drift to sleep, I keep picturing that burned body laid out in the gravel and weeds. It's hard to even think it was a full grown man once with it all shriveled and blackened like that. It looked so frail like it'd disintegrate if you tried to pick it up. And now to know it was the man I watched hover a spoon? Unreal.

Bad guy or not, what the hell is wrong with the world, you know? Setting people on fire and dumping them out in the boonies? My drowsing mind pries around the edges to try to make sense of it, but it can't.

- 5 -

We sit at the snack bar eating soup. It's a coconut based Thai soup with fish sauce, lime juice, cilantro, shiitake mushrooms, and some shrimp. Sounds weird, right? Well, it's not weird. It's delicious. It's like a crazy awesome version of clam chowder where every bite is somehow light and creamy and acidic and a little fishy at the same time. I think Louise got the recipe from Emeril, but I'm not sure.

"Listen," she says. "My client has been in touch."

"Yeah?" I say.

"Yeah," she says. "It's kind of a good news, bad news thing, I guess. See, he offered me a lot of money to look into the Farber murder."

"That sounds pretty good," I say.

"Right, but the thing is," she says. "He also said that the League people know who I am now. Whether it was you blabbing to Babinaux or not, my cover is blown. They know I'm a P.I. and all, and he has doubts about how useful I'll be going forward, as far as working undercover, anyway."

"That sucks," I say. "If it was me, I'm sorry. What are you going to do?"

"Well, I do have one idea. A way you could make it up to me," she says. "But I don't know what you're going to think about it."

She looks so innocent that I'm pretty concerned.

"What is it?" I say.

"Well, I was thinking," she says. "Maybe you could join the League and be my undercover."

"What?" I say. "It's not like I'm going to fly under the radar over there."

"No. I think you've got the wrong idea, Jeffrey. I was there. I've seen how those people talk about you," she says. "They get Jesus eyes. Most of them would be thrilled to hang out with you, let alone have you join them."

"You mean the ones that tossed me in a cell or the other ones?" I say.

"Look, there are other clients and jobs out there. I'm not trying to pressure you or anything," she says. "Just think it over. I thought you might want to do it to see if you could find out anything about where Glenn is."

Argh. I feel guilty and curious and threatened all at once. Mostly threatened, though.

"I'll think about it," I say.

But what I really mean is that I'll think about how I'll never do it.

Days go by, and to her credit, Louise never mentions me joining the League again. There's also no sign of Glenn. Perhaps the oddest development of all - no seizures. No visions transmitted from heavenly places. No metaphysical activity whatsoever. Maybe breaking the cup was a bigger deal than I thought. Maybe I've been cut off. In any case, I'm not all that concerned about it.

In the downtime, I finish cleaning up Glenn's place,

capping the job with a kickass slipcover for the couch. It's houndstooth and looks like it's from the 70's in an awesome way. I've been reading a couple of the books from Glenn's library. Louise comes over a lot in the evenings, and we get a variety of carryout meals and watch movies. Sometimes we kiss a little. Sometimes we kiss a lot. Kind of depends on how good the movie is, I guess.

Anyway, life is more normal than it has been for a long time, and it's awesome. In many respects, in fact, it is better than my life ever was before all of this.

So I'm sure it will all burst into flames any minute now. If life has taught me one lesson, it's that things can never stay like this for long.

- 6 -

I sprawl on the couch in the living room with my legs draped over Louise's lap. She flips through channels on TV, but nothing is on except the news, which seems particularly unfunny tonight. She turns it off.

"I was thinking maybe we'd go out tonight," she says.

"Go out?" I say, sitting up.

"Yeah. Out. Out of this house," she says. "Maybe we could go to this Mexican restaurant, La Pinata, on Lovell Street. It's supposed to be pretty good, but I rarely go over that way, so I've never tried it."

Fuck.

"Hm..." I say. "I don't know if I really feel like it."

"Well, if you're not in the mood for Mexican, we could get something else," she says.

"No," I say. "I meant I'm not in the mood to go out."

She huffs. She doesn't look at me. Her face twists up into a mask of pure evil, but she keeps her malevolent powers directed at the floor.

The crazy thing is that this could have been so much worse. I could have told her that I'm never in the mood to go out. But I played it cool, so this will blow over, and we'll get back to carryout and a movie on Netflix.

Is she infuriated? Absolutely. Is her face engorged with

homicidal rage blood? You know it is. Could she turn on me faster than a Chow turns on its master? If I pushed it, it's almost a certainty.

But I handled it like a pro. I am in the clear in 5, 4, 3-

"No. I don't accept that, Jeffrey. I know you," she says, wheeling the demon cat gaze straight at me. I feel the evil eyes crawling over my skin, hot like those infrared lamps they keep chicken nuggets under in the school cafeteria.

This would be the perfect time to do one of those cool shrugs and downplay all of this, but I don't do that. I panic and freeze like a groundhog in the path of a minivan, my mouth partially open, my nose possibly twitching.

"This is another one of your quirks," she says. I really want to say "she snarls" there, but it'd be an exaggeration. "You push people away, and you coop yourself up like a weird hermit, and I won't stand for it. It's not healthy for person to live like this. Not all of the time."

My instinct is to scurry under the couch and wait for the bad thing to leave. Instead, I twitch my nose a couple more times, flit my eyes around the room and generally remain fastened to my seat.

"So how about this?" she says. "We'll go out once a week. Go to a restaurant or a movie. You'll see that it's not a big deal. And even if it's a little nerve wracking at first, I bet you'll learn to relax and have fun, yeah?"

How cute. The demon is feigning reasonableness to try to confuse me. I close my eyes like that will make this disappear.

"Jeff?" she says.

I squeeze my eyes and jaw and fists shut as hard as I can.

"Are you OK?" she says.

I squeeze and squeeze and squeeze. And something inside my head pops. It feels wet somehow and like a sudden release of a lot pressure, like a cyst bursting in my brain and gushing goo everywhere. I gasp and exhale, and as the air rolls out of me like a receding wave, time slows down a little bit, and I grow more and more relaxed.

The warmth starts at the place where my head meets my neck and spreads outward from there in all directions. What starts as an alleviation of anxiety and tension quickly turns to a tidal wave of bliss washing all up and down me. Every nerve ending, every cell radiates maximized physical pleasure. I guess the only thing I can compare it to is sexual pleasure, but it's more pure than that. Every atom in my body is happy.

It dawns on me that this is a familiar bliss, in fact. I didn't consciously feel it come over me like this on the cot back in the cell, but it surely started this way. I guess with experience I've developed a sensitivity to the process.

I open my eyes to see the world gone white again. My first reaction is to focus right in on my hands. My fingers look like a cross between bratwursts and white caterpillars. I hold them in front of my face and do my jazz hand routine.

Yep. Still hilarious.

Surveying the rest of the room, though, it's not quite the same as it was back in the cell. The walls here almost look like they have a layer of woven spider web stretched across them. Pieces glisten when the light hits the right angle. I swivel my head around to get the full effect.

I glance over at Louise, and she stares back through milk white eyes. Even with all the color drained from her flesh, she doesn't look bad. It's weird. A girl can still be pretty when they

30

turn all white somehow, while I basically look like the great white worm.

"I guess," I say.

It takes a moment for her to respond. I think she senses that something is different about me. Perhaps the jazz hand bit and ensuing fit of giggles were a giveaway. Hard to say.

"You guess?" she says.

"I guess I'll go out to that Mexican place with you," I say.

Truth is, I'm pretty much down to do whatever now that the white world throbs both inside me and outside me. I'm guessing we could walk around the parking lot at a McDonald's, and I'd be thrilled to experience the assortment of sights and sounds.

"OK," she says. "Great. That's great."

She's doing that look again, though, where she turns her head away and squints at me from the corner of her eye. It's a mischievous expression. It reminds me of a Chihuahua that's about two seconds away from latching on to some poor bastard's nose.

I wonder what's going to be on the menu at La Pinata. I bet they'll have Mexican Coca Cola that's made with real cane sugar instead of high fructose corn syrup.

Good.

As.

Hell.

I'm sure they serve burritos, but I bet they have a bunch of other authentic Mexican entrees I've never tried in addition to that. This could get crazy. I'm usually not one to take a chance on something unknown in a restaurant. I play it safe. Maybe it's the chemical bliss beamed into my head from Christ knows where, but today is the day to get a little adventurous, I think.

- 7 -

The restaurant's décor sends mixed messages. The TVs all play soccer with frantic announcers yelling in Spanish while English closed captioning fights to keep up. There's a giant Mexican flag tacked to the back wall, and a few cacti wave hello from behind the counter. On the wall above our booth, however? One of those cardboard Precious Moments cartoons – a very European looking girl with giant blue eyes holding a stuffed rabbit.

I don't get it.

"What do you think?" Louise says. "Seems like a pretty low key place."

I look around, and she's right. It's not super busy. The lighting is dim, which is relaxing, I think. The waitresses are all dressed as casual as possible.

"Yeah," I say. "I can respect that."

The waitress comes to get our drink order. I ask about the Coke. It's legit Mexican, sugar cane and all. Upon confirming this, I do a fist pump like a guy that just scored a touchdown in the Super Bowl.

I start to feel like I'm maybe too excited about this beverage, but then I remember reading that Hitler used to ejaculate during his speeches, and I feel better knowing that there are much weirder people than me out there getting excited about much weirder things. Really excited. I mean, I like a tasty drink, but I've yet to cream my shorts over one.

As I ponder all of this, the waitress returns with the drinks. The fizzy beverage sits before me, looking much paler than usual, naturally. I tear open my straw and shove it down into the bubbly.

Recalling the orange juice incident, I brace myself as I lift the glass toward my mouth and sip at the straw, but I'm still unprepared. The acid stings my tongue, and the carbonation pelts its bubbles at every surface in my mouth. Then the tsunami of sweet hits, and I swear I see rectangles of color imprint themselves on my vision in violent bursts. Every time the colors hit, all sound fades out. Everything returns tinted blue, slowly receding back to white, and I feel like there should be scrolling text at the bottom of my field of vision alerting me to the technical difficulties I'm experiencing. I'm waiting for a disembodied voice to tell me that this is not a test of the emergency broadcast system.

Louise gives me a look as I shake my limp hand out to the side of the table. It's a move I associate with the hero in a movie shortly after he's knocked out the bad guy, but it seems to make sense here all the same.

I point the straw in the Coke away from myself as a precautionary measure and pick up the menu. My eyes pore over every photo, and I read all the descriptions multiple times. I study it like there's going to be an exam when the waitress comes back.

"What are you getting?" I say.

"Chiles Rellenos," Louise says.

"What's that again?" I say, scanning the menu once more.

"It's a roasted poblano pepper stuffed with cheese," she says.

"Oh," I say.

Lunacy!

I order the Bistec Encebollao, which is a Latin style steak in an adobo marinade. I don't know if this was the best choice, but I'm a gambler.

I lose myself watching the text pop up rapid fire at the bottom of the TV screen, and I guess many minutes pass, as the next thing I know, the waitress moves toward us.

The food comes, and steam rises off of everything in dramatic fashion. The waitress sets our meals in front of us and warns us that the plates are hot. Immediately I press the heel of my hand on my plate.

No damage.

My dish looks really good considering the white worm quality and all. After the Coke incident, unfortunately, I'm quite reluctant to eat any of it. I go to work dicing up my meat, so I can at least keep it moving around on the plate. My knife dances it this way and my fork drags it that way. It's like a meat ballet.

"Is everything to your satisfaction, sir?" the waitress says.

"It's great," I say. "Everything's perfect."

I watch her eyes snap to my barely touched plate of food and shift back to me, accompanied by a smirk forming on her lips.

"I'm not feeling well is all," I say.

The waitress nods and shuffles off to refill drinks at the next table.

"You know, for a guy that supposedly doesn't feel well,

you're kind of smiling like a psychopath," Louise says.

As she speaks, I notice something fluttering out from behind her chair. At first I think it's two birds loose in the restaurant, but their flight patterns aren't right, twisting and veering in the air in a way that's unlike the smooth flight pattern of a bird. It's familiar, though.

Bats. They're bats.

Oh shit, I should say something in response to what she said:

"It's hard to explain," I say. "I need to use the restroom, actually."

I watch the bats flutter above me as I stride toward the men's room. They both fly through the ceiling, but I can still see them, if that makes sense. It occurs to me that they're somewhat translucent. Wherever they're flying, there is no ceiling there.

Am I hallucinating now? I must be.

Other shapes start to form around me – trees and bushes leaning and quivering as though the wind is blowing through them, partially translucent like the bats. I don't feel the wind, but I can hear it.

I hustle to the sink and splash cold water on my face like it can wash these visions away. When I open my eyes, however, nothing has changed. I stare at my white worm face in the mirror. I think the bliss alone prevents me from vomiting. My eyes look insane, in any case.

The bathroom door swings open, and an old man walks through, making his way to the urinals. As soon as his back is to me, I rush into a stall and latch the door behind me.

I stand in the poop cubicle, all silent and still. I'm bursting with energy. I want to pace around, but I'm worried this old dude will notice me walking around in the stall and get freaked out. I need to keep a low profile until these visions pass.

So here I am, feigning a deuce in the men's room at La Pinata. I bet this wouldn't have happened if we just stayed home and watched Netflix. Maybe I was right all along about never going out to eat.

The wind noise grows louder, and the leaves on the see through trees and bushes around me kick up again, and it makes an idea pop into my head. Could I be looking into some other dimension? It'd be like being able to see into the alley. My alley, I mean. Almost like I'm half here and half somewhere else.

The flush of the urinal interrupts my thought, followed by the clicks of the soap dispenser and then the water pouring in the sink. After a split second of quiet, the blow dryer kicks on. When that clicks off, silence descends on the room. I hold my breath and listen for a moment.

Not a peep.

Is he gone?

A wet sounding fart rips through the evening and bounces off of every ceramic tile in the room in a tremendous cacophony of fart reverb. And then the bathroom door squeaks open and closed, and the old man ventures off into the night.

With him gone, I'm free to pace in the 15 square foot stall space. It's handicap accessible, so it's roomier than most, I guess.

I walk back and forth, back and forth, my feet following a particular diagonal pattern on the floor tiles. I close my eyes every few seconds, trying to give the ghostly plant life around me the perfect opportunity to fade out discretely. But they don't take the hint. Every time I check, the bushes are still there, waving leaves at me with as much enthusiasm as ever.

I scratch the back of my arm, and after a few swipes, I realize that it feels great. With every nerve ending already singing divine praises, even a touch as basic as a scratch takes it up another notch. I close my eyes and let the scratching move up and down my arm, setting off a million pin pricks of euphoria. I move my fingernails to the back of my neck and go to work on that sensitive spot where the hairline falls. Unbelievable.

My hand slides down my spine, and I scrape and claw and chafe myself to nirvana, the tingle spreading over all of me. I feel like a Christmas tree with all the lights lit up.

And just then I think about Louise sitting out there by herself with my untouched plate of bistec, and I know I can't hang out in here for much longer.

Shit.

I take a couple of deep breaths. I'm not exactly scared, probably thanks in part to the complete and utter bliss. I'm a little overwhelmed, though, almost like the same sensory overload I got from drinking the Coke. When I think about it, there's nothing to indicate that the bats or anything in the tree world can even see me let alone hurt me. I exhale all slowly, counting backward from 10.

I ease open the latch and exit the stall. I stop at the sink for one more face splash of water. As I dab a paper towel across my brow, I hear a whispering voice say:

"Grobnags!"

I freeze, the brown paper still pressed to my forehead. The

voice, definitely a man's, whisper yells again:

"Grobnagger! It's me!"

I lift the paper towel from my face, and it slowly slides out of the frame of my vision like the curtain rising at the start of a play. I gasp as I take in the translucent figure standing in front of me.

It's Glenn.

- 8 -

Glenn squats among some of the see through bushes. Is he hiding? His torso appears noticeably thinner, and an overgrown beard sprouts along his neck and jaw. The disheveled state makes it look like he's right in the middle of morphing into a werewolf.

I wait a second to be sure. He is not morphing into a werewolf.

"Where are you?" I say.

"That's a good question," he says, running his fingers through the new hair under his chin. "I don't have a great answer, and I also don't have long to talk, so let me ask you one instead."

I nod.

"How much time has passed there?" he says.

"Since you walked through the wall?" I say, tilting my head as I tally it up. "Nine days."

"OK, good," he says.

"Why is that good?" I say.

"Well… Time runs differently here," he says. "It's been… a lot longer than that for me, I think. Listen, you need to join the League."

"What?" I say.

"It's important. The League can keep you safe for now," he

says. "And I'll be back... eventually."

As I'm about to ask him if he killed Farber, a kid runs into the restroom followed a few paces later by his dad. I wash my hands and play it all cool. When I look back, Glenn is gone, and the trees and bushes are beginning to flicker in and out.

I run my hands under the blow dryer. It feels awesome. Not quite as good as scratching but close.

I head back out toward the booth where Louise sits. By this time, the trees and the bushes and the wind have all died out. The white world still rages fierce, though, and the euphoria is as strong as ever.

When I get to the table, I see that she already has our leftovers in doggie bags. Really, they are in little plastic containers. It's neither a bag nor in any way affiliated with a dog, but whatever.

The man that feeds his dog leftover food from a Mexican restaurant is the man who deserves to clean up the hurricane of doggie diarrhea headed his way.

She stands as I approach, a somber look occupying her face and mouth. I hug her. I squeeze her close to me and talk softly in her ear:

"Thanks for making me do this."

As I pull back, she smiles a little.

As the Passat nears Glenn's, I stare out the window, so blissed out I almost can't see straight.

"I've been thinking," I say. "About joining the League."

"Really?" Louise says.

I nod.

"It would make a lot of sense, I guess," I say. "I hate to do it in a way, but..."

I don't know why I avoid telling her about talking to translucent Glenn in the Mexican restroom. Aside from the 15 obvious reasons why I would never tell anyone about that, I mean.

I glance toward the driver's seat, and it takes my eyes a second to focus on her face. She has that psychotic look in her eye again.

"You need to make a spectacle of yourself right away," she says.

"Huh?" I say.

"Listen, I know how these people think," she says. "They want something to believe in, something big and dramatic. Just look at Farber with the spoon trick. He had that crowd fawning all over him. They want miracles, Jeffrey, and you're the guy with the divine dreams. You're already just about a legend to them. If you make some dramatic spectacle early on, they'll worship you, and you'll have an easy time getting information."

She's an ambitious lass. I can respect that.

As I brush my teeth and prepare for bed, the color starts to seep back into the world. I'm glad in a way. As it turns out, euphoria can be very tiring.

Plus, as my thoughts begin to clear, I have this weird sense that not knowing how I feel about anything is messing me up. Usually I let my feelings guide me in many ways. When all I feel is unending happiness for hours and hours at a time, it makes it hard to figure out what the hell is going on.

I lie down on the couch and pull the sheet and afghan up to my shoulders. In the half light, I see the covers puff into a bubbled dome that slowly settles on me. Awake in the dark, I keep my eyes open and feel the cool of the sofa slowly warm under me.

As soon as I do close my eyes, a projector rolls in my head and images stream on the insides of my eyelids. Not dreams, exactly, since I'm not asleep, but vivid memories and imaginary bits all mixed together.

I see Glenn huddled in the bushes again. Was he in danger? He didn't say much, really: Time is different wherever he is, and that I should join the League. It was good to see him. I wish he was here to help me.

I never got a chance to tell him about seeing Amity in the alley. I guess it didn't feel like the right time. It's kind of a lot to explain.

The image of Glenn dissolves, and I see my feet walking the diagonal pattern on the ceramic tiles in the bathroom, except with every step I take, the tile lights up as my foot hits it and darkens when I step off. It looks like something in an old music video.

That fades out, and I see Louise at the Mexican restaurant, sitting across the booth from me. She looks bored. It's funny. We sat together, but we were a million miles apart. When I drank that Coke, reality flashed in and out of existence for me, and she had no idea even though she was two feet away. It doesn't seem right in a way, but I don't know what's right, I guess.

The divide between people is weird. We can be close. We can touch, but we're always separate. It feels like we should be able to connect more than that, you know? I don't know. Maybe I just feel this way because I'm messed up at the moment.

For one of us, bats were flying out of the ground and through the ceiling. For the other, it was just a restaurant and a meal.

I don't know. It seems important just now, but I can't say why. Maybe if I knew how I felt about it all the way…

Sometimes I think all of these things, and I wonder if I could be going mad.

- 9 -

In the gray half light of morning, I stand in the front window of Glenn's living room, sipping coffee. Little clouds of fog roll along just above street level. They're only visible in the circles of light beaming down from the street lamps.

Maybe it's some withdrawal symptom now that the white world has left me, but it strikes me as more drab than ever. Weird, right? That the world seems more drab when it returns to full color? That's how it is, though.

Babinaux's Lincoln pulls into the driveway. I'm prepared for once. I went out first thing in the morning and told the dudes in the Impala that follows me around to get a hold of her.

It's weird how silly it seems to demand a meeting like this. It feels like we're all in on a game of pretend spies or something, but then I guess everything about a cult is sort of pretending, right? Or is everything in the world pretending? I guess once someone believes something, it becomes real in a way no matter what it is.

I don't know. Shit starts seeming a lot more real when a burned corpse shows up. I can tell you that much.

I exit the house and patter over the sidewalk to the Lincoln. En route I note that the moon still hangs in the air. It's the shape of a slice of lemon, low on the horizon.

I slide into the backseat. Babinaux wears some kind of black skirt suit with a satin blouse the color of eggplant underneath. She always looks ready to cross-examine a witness or something.

"Good morning, Jeffrey," she says.

"Hi," I say. "I want to join the League."

She tucks her chin into her neck, I guess out of surprise. It makes a bunch of weird folds in the under chin region, and it looks like she has no chin. She should avoid doing this. Maybe everyone should.

"Really?" she says.

"Yes," I say.

"Can I ask why?" she says.

I splay my fingers over my mouth as I consider the best words to spin this answer into a positive light.

"Because something is happening to me, and the League probably knows more about it than anyone else," I say. "Plus, I think you guys could protect me."

She hesitates, nods.

"I can let the right people know and make the proper arrangements," she says, her chin slowly reappearing. "How are you, though? You look a little puffy around the eyes."

I feel around my eyelids. I do feel a little swollen.

"I'm fine," I say. "Things have been a little weird, I guess. You remember how I told you that the world was bled white while I was in the cell? It happened again last night."

"Interesting," she says. "Is it scary?"

"Not really," I say. "I mean, I'm basically high, so I'm just really happy."

"What led to it happening this time?" she says.

"Well, Louise was pressuring me to go out to eat," I say. "I was getting frustrated, and I did this move where I clenched up, and it was like something popped in my head. I think I can probably do it at will. Haven't tested that yet, but I think so."

Babinaux rolls her neck.

"She was pressuring you?" she says. "You two are dating, I take it?"

"Yeah. And I hate going out to eat," I say. "She was busting my balls about it pretty good."

Her lips purse into something just shy of bitter beer face.

"You know," she says. "You're supposed to be with somebody that makes you feel good."

"Well," I say. "Yeah. What?"

"Maybe I'm reading into things, but if she's putting all of this pressure on you…" she says.

"Oh. No, I probably did a bad job of describing it," I say. "So how will this work? With the League, I mean. Is there like a clubhouse or something?

"There's a compound," she says.

Wow. This cult is legit.

"I'm just kidding," she says. "We mostly meet at people's houses in small groups. Every week or two there are bigger gatherings at an old church we have on Spring Street. The building is not in the best shape or we'd probably utilize it more frequently."

I am beginning to detect a pattern with this old hospital and old church being in disrepair. They like buying things but not necessarily doing the work required to make them useful. Interesting. I'm not sure if that's a quality I'm looking for in the people I make responsible for protecting me, but I can relate to the path of least resistance ethos.

"Once I make some calls, I'll let you know when and where you'll be making your first appearance," she says. "But if you want some advice? Keep your head down. With all the talk about your dreams, you're going to draw a lot of attention at first, but if you leave well enough alone, all of that will pass and things can be normal."

"Sounds good," I say.

But really what it sounds like is the opposite of what Louise suggested.

- 10 -

None of this seems real.

I pull on the maroon robe. It and the matching pants are both crafted of a shiny fabric that reflects yellow wherever the light catches it. It looks like it would be the perfect material for curtains in a king's bedroom or something. Regal as hell.

I'm the only one left in the little dressing room. Everyone else is out in the nave waiting to get this thing kick started.

According to Babinaux, because of my reputation, the higher ups want to put me on the "fast track." Apparently that means I will go through the "blood ritual" tonight. They only do it every six months, so they wanted to squeeze me in now rather than wait.

I guess for the average member, you wouldn't go through with this bad boy until your mentor feels you're ready, and this usually takes months if not years. Jeff Grobnagger gets the express pass, though.

Boom.

Babinaux said someone would walk me through the details, but this didn't happen. Instead everybody just walked out of the room upon my arrival, so I'm going in blind.

I cinch the belt around my waist, but the chest area keeps coming loose and exposing my dumb nipples. I adjust everything, re-tie the belt and seem to get it under control.

I throw the hood up over my head. It's the oversized style made popular by the grim reaper. I check myself out in the mirror. So long as you can't see my nipples, I actually look pretty intimidating, I think. The hood does a lot of the heavy lifting in that regard.

I walk out toward the main chamber of the church, past a row of arched stained glass windows. I assume they depict churchy things, but I can't tell in the dark. The only light is provided by a shit ton of candles. If I had to guess, I'd say they cleaned out an entire Pottery Barn.

A bunch of hooded heads snap away from me as soon I set foot across the threshold of the door, and then they all freeze in that position, faced away.

I see how it is. I'm the freak show everybody wants to sneak a peek at without getting caught. I take a seat in the back row. There are maybe 30 people in the pews in front of me.

Up in the sanctuary, a guy with a white beard and a medallion hanging from his neck carries a goblet up to an altar and places it there. He kind of looks like Dumbledore, so I assume this is the Goblet of Fire.

He stands facing us, his arms raised above the cup resting between him and all of us. After a silent moment of rapturous facial expression, he speaks.

"We gather here, a League dedicated to answers of the spirit, the light that shines in us all," he says. "We seek not power. We seek not wealth. We seek only an understanding of the light."

He picks up a dagger from the altar and holds it up. It's ornate – both the blade and the hilt are curved. The blade is sort of a wiggly shape, the kind I associate with a cartoon dagger.

"We spend our time, we spend our lives, we spend our blood on this journey. The sacrifice is great, but the light is greater than all in this realm," he says. "Would thou join us on this quest?"

Voices rise from the crowd in unison:

"I shall join you."

He touches the palm of his left hand to the tip of the dagger and then holds it up facing us. I'm too far back to see whether or not he broke the skin, but this is getting a little weird.

"With this blade, spill thine blood," he says.

Uh-oh.

Dumbledore points, and a guy in the first row rises and walks to the altar. He lifts the dagger to his wrist and drags it across his skin, arm suspended over the goblet. I sit forward, squinting. He switches hands and drags it across the other wrist. Then he sets the dagger down and drinks.

I don't think he cut himself, though. I think he pantomimed it. Maybe these guys are half-assed in areas beyond fixing up the real estate they get ahold of.

The man returns to his seat, sneaking an angry glare at me just before he sits. I better watch out. He might pretend to stab me.

The next guy goes up, mimes a wrist slash, drinks some pinot noir and sits down. And then the next, and then the next.

As the procession of fake bleeding moves through the pews from front to back, I get more dirty looks. A red headed lady scowls at me, a guy with a shaved head tries to stare me down but blinks and looks away, the hooded heads in the crowd sway and bob and rubberneck my way. Everybody wants to have a quick stare at ol' Grobnags.

Yeah? Well, if they want a freak show, I'll give them a goddamn freak show. I'll give them something they'll understand.

Sitting in the back of the room, I'm up last. I stride to the altar, my head down. When I reach the sanctuary, I turn to face the crowd. Only a couple of the weirdos dare to make eye contact: a heavyset lady that seems a little oblivious and a guy that looks remarkably like that professional wrestler the Undertaker. He looks at me with contempt. Everyone else makes a more or less hostile expression as well, but they won't look directly at my face.

They don't want none.

I lift the dagger and hold the opposite hand over the goblet. I hesitate, watching all of the hoods lean forward to see me spill imaginary blood.

Instead, I pull the top of my robe open. I bring the knife to my chest and take a breath. The blade etches a line there diagonally just above my sternum, and then carves another diagonal going the other way. The sharpness of it stings at first, but then I only really have the sensation of cutting thick paper in a weird way. As I move the dagger away, I watch the flaps of skin pull apart from each other in slow motion like two sheets of fleshy fabric. I feel opened up, the air touching my insides.

The blood trickles out of every part of the X at once, oozing thick and gummy red. Rivulets leak down from the corners. It moves slowly like the streams of water about to get erased by the windshield wipers.

Before I look up, the silence in the room surrounds me. There are no words. There are no gasps. I'm not even sure anyone is breathing.

And in the quiet, it becomes real. The violence of the act sinks in. The drama of it all strikes me. And it occurs to me suddenly that this is exactly like something I would have done in the alley and never ever done in real life… until just now, anyway.

I look up to see all eyes locked on the crossed lines above my heart. Jaws hang open. Hands clutch at chests and cup lips.

I hold the goblet up to the bloody well springs and let the fluid drain from my torso into the cup for a bit. It's not so much blood, really – maybe a couple of ounces, maybe not even that. I smear my fingers in the red and wipe them across my brow, following that stroke with a perpendicular line down my forehead and onto my nose.

I wait for that Undertaker looking bastard to make eye contact. Nothing moves for a beat as he gazes at my injury like everyone else. Finally, he senses my stare and returns it, but he looks frightened now. Once we lock eyes, I raise the goblet to my lips and drink, long and cool. It's a sloppy swig, the wine running out of both sides of my mouth and down my chin. I can't even taste the blood. It just tastes like Riuniti or some other cheap wine.

I plop the goblet back down on the altar, wipe the drink off of my chin with my sleeve and smile a moment. I wait. I want this image to linger. Then I return to my seat.

Nobody moves for a long time. I return to my seat in the back and watch the backs of their idiot heads.

Eventually, they stand and mill around and shuffle out, guffawed and dismayed and unhappy. I sit with my arms crossed over my wound, and no one dares to look at me.

Isn't this what they all wanted? Now they can get all scared and aroused and believe in magic and shit. They can gather around water coolers with some juicy new story to share. They can lie in bed quivering and wonder about it and dream about it and fear it.

I mean, I'm sure this was pretty intimidating, even if they could see my nipples.

I lie on my back on the couch, awake in the dark again. I tried to call Louise when I got home, but she didn't answer, so I decided to go to bed early.

With the lack of light, I can barely make out the rectangle of white bandage taped to my chest. The dull ache in the trunk of my body isn't what keeps me up, though. It's the one inside my head. Where the pain comes from, I can't even say.

I replay the event time and again. I see my blood flowing. I watch their faces, their sneers. But I don't really feel the same wrath toward them that I did. I'm not so hateful now. I just feel separate from everything.

And as those pictures play, my thoughts descend to that place they haven't been in a while, the endless circles of words that turn everything into nothing - the big nothing. The words spiral themselves into weapons that attack everyone else to get me alone, and once all the others are defeated, they turn on me.

I try to reason my way out of it. I try to fight against the words, but I can't. They know me too well. They know every scab to pick at. They know how to win every argument. They know how to twist me around and make me think whatever they want.

So I clench my jaw, and I squeeze my eyes shut. My fists

ball up, and for a second I feel small and powerless. For one second I am nowhere and nobody, and then the bubble in my head pops, and I feel the juice gush out.

And I watch in the dark as the ceiling fades to white above. And heaven opens in my head, and I disconnect from the bad thoughts in a flash. I wouldn't say they're erased for good, but they are erased for now.

The despair disintegrates. Warm and calm, I fall asleep within 90 seconds.

- 11 -

A horn blasts, and I'm awake. I sit up, confused, my hands balled into fists out of instinct. I look around. The world hasn't quite returned to full color yet. It blares again – a car horn out front.

I rise and peek through the curtains. Babinaux's Lincoln waits in the driveway.

Oh, shit. She was supposed to pick me up to go to some League house meeting and to start talking to some of these people in earnest. I guess I slept in. I scramble to dress myself in yesterday's clothes lying in a pile nearby, the wound on my chest stinging momentarily as I pull on the t-shirt.

I scratch my brow on the way to the door and feel something rough in texture like dried spaghetti residue on a plate. Oh, the dried blood still crusted to my forehead. I guess I forgot about that.

I stick my face under the kitchen faucet for a quick rinse and scrub my fingers at my brow until it feels smooth. I head out to the car.

In an alarming display of her all-knowingness, Babinaux wordlessly hands me a paper cup of coffee as I slide into the backseat. I sip, and it's not just coffee. It's some kind of delicious cinnamon concoction, perhaps a little too sweet, but I'm not looking a gift coffee in the mouth hole. Within a few seconds, I'm already perking up.

"Everyone is talking again. You made quite the first impression last night," she says. I can see her eyes crawling all over my face to try to read me.

"It was a weird time," I say.

She nods and looks out the window.

"I worry about you," she says.

"I'm fine," I say. "I can't really remember why I did it."

"That's not what I meant," she says. "I worry about more than just that."

"Either way," I say. "I'm fine."

"I hope that's true," she says.

She looks at me for a long time, and then reaches into her purse. She pulls out a plastic bottle and tumbles three pills into her palm. She reaches toward me, and I open my hand, receiving another gift.

"What's this?" I say, rubbing the capsules between my fingers. They're full of green.

"It's Kava Kava," she says. "It's an herb that helps with anxiety. Don't worry, it's really mild."

"Thanks," I say. I wash them down with the cinnamon sludge from the bottom of the cup.

We arrive, and I climb out of the car. The house looks like a cartoon villain lives in it. Ivy devours the chimney and sends green tendrils snaking out to cover most of the upstairs windows.

Standing on the doorstep, I take a breath. I'm here to dig up dirt about Farber's murder, I remind myself. Nothing else matters. None of these people matter to me. I don't have to be nervous. I just have to wait for the right time to ask some questions.

A sign on the front door says, "Come on in!"

So I do that.

A glare on the window prevents me from being able to see inside. I expect to hear Cruella Deville cackling from somewhere deep within the bowels of the building, but instead the only thing I hear is the door screeching super loud as I open it. A group of six people huddled around a snack bar near the front door wheel around to face me.

I stop in the doorway, light shining from behind me so my face is partially in shadow.

"Hi," I say.

"Hey Jeff," the guy that looks like Dumbledore says. "My name's Randy. Randy Pittaway. Can I interest you in a pumpkin scone?"

He shoves the pointy end of a scone in my direction in a way that seems a little too aggressive, but I don't know. Maybe he's just passionate about baked goods.

"Sure," I say.

Now, obviously I'd prefer to take one of the scones on the platter in front of him - you know, one of the ones he hasn't smeared his greasy mitts all over – but I take the one from his hand for the sake of politeness. I bite it, and it tastes more like pumpkin than hand, so I guess that's a win.

"Tasty," I say, everyone watching me chew.

"Vegan recipe," he says. "I baked them fresh this morning."

See? I knew this guy was passionate about baked goods.

I try to make an impressed face. He seems pleased, so I guess it worked. An older lady with dyed black hair next to him speaks up.

"We've heard so much about you," she says. "I'm Janice."

We shake hands. At this point, I'm bombarded from all angles with handshakes and introductions. It's kind of overwhelming, so I don't register any of the names after Janice. They are kind to me, though, and it seems genuine enough.

The standout among the group is a guy with glasses and really hairy ears – like a puff of curly hair actually sticking out from each of his ears. Not unlike pubic hair in texture, as a matter of fact. Ear beards, I guess you could call them. I think maybe his name is Will... possibly Todd.

"I have a question for you, Mr. Grobnagger," Dumbledore says. Randy, I mean. Shit. I hope I don't accidentally call him Dumbledore out loud at some point.

"What's that?" I say.

"Do you eat meat?" he says.

"Only at, like, pretty much every meal," I say.

There are a few chuckles from the snack bar, Janice the loudest among them.

"Do you have any pets?" he says.

"Yeah, I have a cat," I say.

"Would you kill it and eat it?" he says.

"Nope," I say.

"What if you were starving?" he says.

"No," I say. "He weighs like 10 pounds, and I figure most of that is bone. It wouldn't make enough of a difference to be worth it."

"Do you think you'd be able to kill a cow if that's what it took to eat a cheeseburger?" he says.

I imagine myself jamming a knife into a cow's throat and

slashing, blood spraying like a fountain. Then I imagine it again, and this time I just pat the cow on the head.

"Nope," I say.

He squints at me and nods and then looks away. They go on talking about animals and spirits and such. I guess that's the topic of the day, though I'm not 100% clear on how all of this works.

Anyway, once the attention is off of me I relax a bit and zone out. Maybe the kava kava kicked in or something, but it's pretty cool in any case. I take a seat in an antique rocking chair in the corner, happy to be off in my own world.

I watch out the window as a bird picks up clumps of dried grass, flies off with them, and then comes back for more. Must be building a nest. It's a finch, I think.

Snippets of the conversation filter through to my consciousness, particularly during the moments when the bird is away:

"It's not about that," Randy says. "It's about blocking out the animal urges that constantly clutter our thoughts, stripping away those shallow wants and desires and trying to truly understand our existence in the moment. Once we do that, we realize that so much of our experience is shared among all of the creatures walking around out there. That the things we think and feel and do are largely universal."

Later the guy with the hairy ears, Will or whatever, says:

"Surely a clam can't have emotions or consciousness. Look, I'm more than willing to stop eating steak and pork chops, but once we work our way down the food chain to clam chowder, I no longer get the point of abstaining. Is anyone seriously suggesting that a clam has complex feelings?"

I thought for sure someone would reply, "I am serious…
and don't call me Shirley," but no one did.

Someone passes around the tray of scones, so I indulge.
They taste better when you're not thinking about whether or
not there's residue from Dumbledore's balls all over them.
Damn it! Randy's balls, I mean. Randy's balls! I've got to
remember that.

The bird pecks like crazy at the bark at the bottom of an
Oak tree. Not sure what he's playing at. And suddenly I realize
that the room is silent, and the last thing said was my name a
few seconds ago.

"Hm?" I say, rotating my head to face everyone.

The whole group looks at me with these wide eyed
expressions that remind me of the face a mom would make at a
toddler after their first day of preschool.

"I suppose Jeff wouldn't want to dive right into regaling us
with dreams on day one," Randy says. "Let's all give him time
to get acclimated to our little group before we start bombarding
him with questions, OK?"

OK wait. Maybe the kava kava is slowing me down here,
but I start putting the puzzle pieces together. So someone must
have asked about my dreams, and my not hearing the question
resulted in me not having to answer it.

That.

Is.

Awesome.

I should probably keep that trick up my sleeve for future
use. Pretending to not hear what someone said. Genius.

They go back to yakking, and I go back to finch watching.
Somewhere along the way, time speeds up, and suddenly the

group is standing up and gathering their things. I guess it's over already.

Everyone makes a point of saying bye to me. Janice hugs me – one of those strange hugs where I can distinctly feel her saggy breasts squishing into me.

Will claps me on the shoulder and says:

"Really glad to have you here this week. We all hope you come back."

The crowd thins, and before long, it's just me and Randy. He wipes down the snack bar with a rag. I guess this is my shot.

"It's too bad about Farber, eh?" I say.

I pull out the nonchalant shrug and give that a whirl. I can leave nothing to chance here.

"Yeah," he says. "Too bad, indeed."

He looks up from the partially wiped countertop to meet my eyes. His expression is hard to read. I want to say forlorn here, but I don't remember what that means for sure. I have earned like three college credits in my lifetime, so I know almost nothing.

"Seems like there's something you want to tell me about it," I say.

Total stab in the dark. Randy sighs.

"So you're as perceptive as they all say you are," he says. "I do have thoughts about the murder, but they're just that – thoughts. I don't make a habit of speculating about such things. And I'd rather not start. Not yet, anyway."

I ponder this a moment.

"People say I'm perceptive?" I say. "Like who?"

"Marcy Babinaux talks about you like you're her only son and you're some kind of violin prodigy or something," he says.

"And I guess the others parrot those sentiments."

Her first name is Marcy? Weird.

"I will say that I saw your passion first hand, and it was jarring," he says. "But impressive."

He might as well be speaking Parseltongue.

"What?" I say.

"Taking the dagger to your chest last night," he says. "To perform the blood ritual the ancient way. I knew from the stories that you were fairly adept at most things metaphysical, but I got the impression that you were fairly indifferent toward it. I had no idea you were a true student of the occult with such a fire in your heart for it."

I don't say anything. Randy sweeps the crumbs from the edge of the counter into his cupped hand and tosses them in the trash.

"That alone gives me hope for the future," he says. "Now that you've elected to join us, anyhow."

I continue to not say anything. I look out the window, but the finch is long gone. He probably caught wind of this conversation and flew South to avoid the awkwardness.

After a long moment of silence, I think of a way to change the subject.

"Oh hey," I say. "What can you tell me about Farber's disciples? Are the stories about Seth Cromwell true?"

Randy's eyes go wide.

"I do not speak his name," he says, whispering. "Perhaps that should tell you whether or not I believe the stories to be true."

He clears his throat.

"I've always been much more uneasy around *him* than I

ever was around Farber," he says. "You just sense a violence about him. I've known his type in the past, desperate men. His ilk share a lust for power, but it's a hateful lust that wields its power only in destruction."

He stares off into space a moment.

"We best get going," Randy says, draping the rag over the side of the sink.

I grab a scone for the road.

- 12 -

Randy gives me a ride home in his Prius. Though on the whole the excursion wasn't as nerve wracking as I anticipated, I still feel quite relieved to be done with it – just shy of euphoric. It's like when you've been dreading going to the dentist forever. Once it's finally over, you feel like some kind of champion.

When I walk in the door, Louise is already there waiting for me. She sits on the couch, an afghan draped over her lap.

"How did it go?" she says.

"Not as bad as I figured," I say.

"Did you make any progress?" she says.

"Not really, but Dumbledore knows something," I say, sliding my shoes off. "He said he doesn't want to talk about it, so it might take a while to pry it out of him. Either way, I figure that's better than nothing."

"That's great," she says. "You know, I always figured you'd be pretty good at getting people to talk. You're not a bullshitter. People talk to people they think are being real, and a lot of people, maybe most, never are."

She stands and smiles, and the blanket falls away revealing that only underwear clothe her bottom half. For a second, I am frozen, watching her. Nothing else in the universe exists but her. She walks to the bedroom in slow motion. And as she crosses the threshold, moving out of sight, real time snaps back, and I unfreeze.

I am in there in a flash.

She crawls into the bed, and as I follow she says:

"No pants allowed."

I undress down to my boxers. Without thinking about it, I take off my shirt as well.

I climb under the sheet with her. We kiss a moment, but she pulls away. Her fingers caress the bandage on my chest.

"What happened?" she says.

"Well, I made a spectacle of myself… like you wanted, I guess," I say.

"Let me see," she says.

She pries the corner of the bandage free with great care and peels it open. The scabbed X underneath puckers angry red.

She gasps a little, and her eyelashes flutter. Then she leans forward and kisses it. Her touch is light, so it doesn't sting or anything. In fact, I can barely feel it at all.

She reattaches the bandage over my heart and then leans back and strips off her shirt.

Holy shit. There are boobs… and stuff. I don't know. It's hard to concentrate on words just now.

Kissing. Touching. Her skin brushes against mine, and I feel the goose bumps crawl across her. She is the softest thing I have ever felt.

Time changes. I can't decide if it speeds up or slows down, but it's definitely different. I am here, and I am somewhere else at the same time. I am nowhere and everywhere. I am nothing. I am connected to something bigger than myself.

At some point in there, a sweet make out session becomes a sweet do it session.

She writhes on top of me, and the volume of existence gets turned up. And we are beyond ourselves, beyond human. We are more like animals and more like spiritual beings at the same time somehow.

And part of me can't believe that this is a real living person lying with me. She is alive. She is conscious. Her imagination is an endless well of pictures and dreams and memories just like mine. And we are, in some way, joined for a while.

It is too big to comprehend. I can't quite accept it as real.

It feels tremendous, though. I will give it that.

Later that night, I lie awake in the dark, Louise dozing next to me. I can't sleep, so my mind reaches out into the blackness.

It does that.

I look over, and I can see Louise's face, a white glow in the shadows. I can't make out all of the details, but I can see the half smile of sleep on her lips.

And part of me finds great satisfaction in all of this. Romance and companionship and sex and everything. I mean, I got the girl I want, you know? Being with her is the most exciting thing that has happened to me in a long time.

But another part of me feels only a greater emptiness than ever. That my whole existence in some way revolves around those three seconds bothers me. Not on a rational level, on a feeling level.

As a man, my imagination, my emotions, my thoughts and dreams, in some way boil down to a desire to breed, to spread my seed, to jizz, whatever you want to call it. Most every moment of every day comes back to that. I don't mean that in a "men think of sex all of the time" raunchy way so much as on a subconscious level. Like I got good at poker and made money and had this sense of conquest, but isn't glory seeking just a way to prove yourself a worthy mate? Isn't acquiring wealth the same? Doesn't every guy that picks up a guitar want to meet a girl? Isn't every stand up comic braving the risk of bombing and embarrassing the fuck out of himself for the mere chance to prove their wit and skill to the ladies?

We are driven to make our lasting mark on the species.

Sometimes this instinct gets subverted into more of a general legacy thing. Guys like Donald Trump build huge towers with their name plastered on them in giant letters. But it comes from the same place. He wants his lasting mark to be in the physical world instead of the species, but I think it's just a confused version of the real impulse. I mean, huge towers are on the phallic end of the spectrum, no?

All of our time and efforts and thoughts and skills get poured into this, whether we realize it or not. And if we're lucky, we get there. We get the girl we desire. We prove ourselves worthy.

And so the sex act happens. And all of the feelings build up into something sacred, some sense of being connected not only to a woman but to heavenly bodies above, some belief that everything finally makes sense. All of the pieces of the universe slide into place, and it satisfies beyond comprehension.

For 3 seconds life has meaning.

And once it's over, you realize there's really nothing. That all of your identity, your imagination and thoughts and dreams, that spark of divine madness that makes each of us unique - they are all just functions of a brain serving an animal urge to keep the species going, no different from the urges that an ape has or even an insect. More elaborate, perhaps, but of the same essence.

And if the urge gets its way, you will produce kids that live to serve those same urges and on and on. And maybe that's all we really are, and all else is an illusion.

I don't know. Part of me thinks that, I guess.

I look over at Louise, and I want to believe otherwise. I want to feel something else entirely. I stare up toward the ceiling, but there's no guiding light to be found up there – only the black nothing.

And then I glance over at her again and her eyes are open. She sees my head tilt in her direction and mumbles something.

"What?" I say.

"I said I want a milkshake," she says.

"What? It's the middle of the night," I say.

"I want," she says. "A milkshake."

We sit on the couch, milkshakes in hand. Turns out Louise makes a damn good shake. She even used real vanilla beans, slitting down the side and scraping the insides out. Mind blowing.

I explained the cutting incident to her in greater detail in the kitchen between blender blasts, pantomiming some of the dramatic moments with a spatula playing the role of the dagger. Replaying it got me thinking about something Randy said.

I pull her laptop off of the coffee table and get to Googling. If she ever gets charged with a crime, it'll be hilarious for the police to find all of these searches about blood rituals in her browser history.

"OK check this out," I say. "Aleister Crowley had a technique that involved cutting your chest like I did as part of a blood ritual. It's called the Mass of the Phoenix."

"That's interesting," Louise says, flipping through infomercials on TV.

"It says something about eating a 'Cake of Light,'" I say. "I definitely did not see any refreshments that evening. That's one thing I would remember."

"What the hell is a Cake of Light?" Louise says.

I look it up.

"Says it's a wafer made from meal, honey, olive oil, oil of Abremalin – whatever the hell that is – and blood or other bodily fluids," I say.

My eyebrows go way up, and Louise's mimic the gesture.

"Yikes!" she says.

I search further.

"We have semen!" I say. "Apparently, they eat their own sperm… in cake form. Though, I guess there are probably worse forms. Like I bet sperm burgers aren't that great."

Louise gags on milkshake and laughs super hard. She sounds a little hoarse.

"I wonder if they were at all bashful about that," I say. "Like, 'Listen, guys, let's maybe not tell my mom about the sperm cakes. I was thinking that would just kind of stay between us cult members.'"

Louise topples onto her side, and her face turns all red, tears wetting her cheeks. Silent laughs rattle her ribcage with great force. It sort of looks like the chestburster scene in Alien.

"Why sperm?" she manages to hiss out.

I read on.

"Says here it's for the robust flavor," I say.

"What?" she says.

"Just kidding," I say. "It's a eucharist. The cake symbolizes the union between man and the divine. Eating it confirms the connection between the two and strengthens the bond. Like communion in a way, I guess. Really gross communion."

Louise's laughing slows, and she does some of those gasp sobs. It sounds like when a baby can't stop crying.

"Jesus. It says of the blood options, moon blood is the best. I assume that means menstrual blood?" I say, "So yeah. That cements it. Aleister Crowley – worst pastry chef ever."

The next night, I look up from my book to see the headlights in the driveway again - Babinaux's Lincoln. Maybe I should invite her in for once. I wonder why I never thought of this until just now.

I walk out to the car in the half light of dusk. The moon looks down, shaped like an egg. I open the door to the backseat.

"Hey, you want to come inside?" I say.

A look of mild confusion crinkles her eyebrows. I think this concept had never occurred to her, either.

"Sure," she says.

Inside, she sits on the couch while I pour a couple of Arnold Palmers. After much experimenting with the various brands and varieties Glenn has on hand, I've figured out that I like an Arnold Palmer made with Meijer brand green tea best. It's one of the cheapest teas available, but I prefer it to any other. I call it "Grobnag's Nothin' Fancy Arnold Palmer." I describe all of this to Babinaux in great detail as I prepare the beverage. For some reason, I can't shut up about it.

"So how has everything been?" she says, once my mouth finally pauses for a few seconds.

"Pretty good," I say. "Randy seems like an interesting guy. He makes a killer pumpkin scone. Very passionate about baked goods, that one."

She smiles.

"Have you had any… seizures… or…?" she says.

"No seizures," I say. "It's been a low key time."

I think about how I never told her, or anyone else, about seeing Glenn in the white world, but I don't think there'd be much point now.

"Yeah, aside from carving your chest like a thanksgiving turkey, it's been pretty laid back, huh?" she says.

"OK, that's a good point," I say.

"Things good with your girlfriend?" she says.

I sip my drink before I answer.

"Yeah," I say. "I mean, it doesn't even feel all the way real most of the time."

"What do you mean?" she says.

"I don't know," I say. "It's hard for me to process that a real person is with me, wants to be with me. Does that make sense?"

Her eyes flick to the side, and she does a cautious half tilt of her head.

"Maybe," she says. "Like when? Give me an example."

I think about it.

"A specific example?" I say. "I don't know. It's hard to call one to mind just like that."

"Let me rephrase my question: Do you mean during sex?" she says.

I lean back, my shoulders digging into the couch cushions.

"Sheesh," I say. "I didn't know you were going to leap straight for the jugular."

"I'm sorry. If you're not comfortable talking about that…" she says.

"No, it's fine," I say. "And yeah, I think that's a pretty good example of what I meant. It's not the only time, but yeah. Yeah."

She strokes her cheek in thought, staring off into space.

"I think I understand, then," she says. "I knew someone like you once, a long time ago. He detached like that in intimate moments, sexual or otherwise. It wasn't a conscious effort to escape or anything. It wasn't that he didn't like the people close to him. He just couldn't absorb it – that connection between people. Too intense, I think, for someone that sensitive. It overwhelmed him."

I don't know what to say.

"He was the saddest person I ever knew. Even as a kid," she says.

She shakes her head, and her eyes don't look so far away after.

"It's weird," she says. "I haven't smoked a cigarette in years, but I just got the urge for one. I guess thinking about old times jars your brain and the old habits shake loose."

I have a hard time imagining her smoking. She seems too classy for that.

She brings her hand to her mouth and nudges the side of her index finger into her lips. I don't know if that's because she's thinking about cigarettes or what.

- 13 -

At the next meeting at Randy's there are tasty wafer cookies filled with coconut and lemon cream. Delicious. I grab another from the tray. I want to grab three, but I decide to play it cool and take one at a time.

At first I thought they must not be vegan, but I think the cream is coconut oil based maybe. Randy Pittaway is to dessert what Albus Dumbledore is to magic.

I sit in my rocking chair in the corner and watch the people talk. I don't necessarily listen the whole time, but I do watch. The corner of Janice's mouth twitches. She seems preoccupied.

I can't be sure, but I think Will might have trimmed his ear beards. They're still there, but they have a more manicured look, like the bushes outside of a fancy hotel.

Piecing together bits of the conversation, Randy seems to be attempting to discuss spiritual clarity. I can hardly stand to listen to even one complete sentence of it, though, so I can't be sure. My brain shuts down all aural functions when it hears certain keywords, and Randy is hitting them pretty hard today. I must not be alone in my lack of interest, however, because Janice keeps going off topic.

"I wanted Kim, that's my son's fiancée, to wear my mama's wedding dress like I did, but she insists she will need to pick out her own," Janice says. "Now, I don't want to press it and make a scene, but my goodness! Whatever happened to tradition and family coming first? Is that era of America just flushed down the commode?"

Janice has a slight Southern accent, but I think she might be one of those people that inexplicably employs a twang even though she's never lived in the South. It seems like most of them say po-lice, too. Fun fact.

Everyone is silent.

"I know where you're coming from, Janice," Randy says, tapping his fingers on his mug. "That kind of ties into what I'm talking about, because I think we'd all be more chill if we stopped listening to all the noise outside and set aside quiet time to pay attention to the light inside."

Chill? I immediately vomit lemon and coconut all over the snack bar.

Well... not really, but damn near. Randy seems like a nice guy, but I don't know why he has to get all Dudley Do-Right in these group meetings. I take a bite of a cookie, and the coconut cream squirts into my mouth.

I freeze. Visions of sperm cakes dance in my head. I look at Randy, this saint of dessert-hood before me. Could there be an ulterior motive to his passion for desserts?

I cup a napkin to my mouth and feign a cough, spitting the cream out.

If Randy has done the unthinkable... let's just say that ain't vegan.

After the meeting dies down, and the others stream out into the sunlight, I find a way to ask him about it.

"So these cookies," I say.

"Did you like them?" he says, gathering up stray dishes

from the counter.

"Yeah. They're great, but I have a question," I say.

I pause for a beat.

" These wouldn't be in anyway 'Cakes of Light' or anything like that, right?" I say.

"What?" he says as he places some dirty mugs in the sink.

I say nothing. I let the question hover in the space between us and try to watch his face for micro expressions like a detective in a murder of the week TV show. His face does change, but it's no fleeting micro expression. It lights up with shock – eyes wide, mouth agape.

"Oh!" he says. "Oh, lord no! Wait. You thought… ?"

He busts out laughing, his hands falling to the corner of the counter. After a second, he bends at the waist and rests his head on his hands. Tears fall from his eyes and spatter on his glasses.

He has one of those crazy laughs that sounds louder on the inhale than the exhale. It has a wheezy quality to it.

I don't think I've ever seen an old person laugh like this. He looks like a maniac. I mean, I know laughter is supposed to be the best medicine, but Randy is flirting with an overdose at this point.

I wipe down the counter while I wait for this episode to pass. Randy's wheeze slows and eventually peters out, but he keeps his head down a while longer. I eye the cookies while I wait for his recovery, but I can't bring myself to eat one. Even though I know they've been cleared for consumption, I would just think about sperm while I ate them, so…

Randy finally stands up. He gives me a look and shakes his head. The corners of his mouth flutter, and for a second I think he's going to go relapse back into giggles, but he holds it

76

together.

He slides the leftover cookies off of a tray into a Tupperware container and pops it in the fridge. I figure now is the time to make with the interrogation.

"Heard anything new about the Farber case?" I say.

He stops in his tracks, and his chest heaves once with a deep breath. He holds his eyes closed for a beat before he speaks.

"I have mixed feelings about it, but I'm going to tell you what I know, and what I fear it means," he says. "I think in some way you will play a big role in all of this, Grobnagger, so concealing information from you might be unwise."

I bob my head a single time, and he continues.

"Rumor has it that Farber acquired a book of great power recently," he says. "I believe you're already aware of that. Well, I happen to know a bit about the book. There's a passage – an incantation – regarding the final rituals for achieving divinity on Earth. It involves a final display of faith, see. This particular ritual ends with a trial by fire."

I wait for him to go on, but the words hang in the air. He just looks at me.

"What are you saying?" I say.

"I'm saying Farber lit himself on fire to prove his faith. To become a God on Earth," he says. "He failed it seems, so that's not what worries me about it. What worries me is that his ilk remains out there, likely the Sons of Man, and they will continue to try."

"So the bad guys are burning themselves to death," I say. "I think that's kind of a good thing."

"Sooner or later, one of them will get it right, Grobnagger," he says. "And believe me, we'll all be up shit creek at that point."

We're quiet for a moment. I imagine myself wielding a turd paddle, fighting against the frothy rapids of shit creek.

"What's with the name, anyway?" I say.

"The name?" he says.

"The Sons of Man," I say.

"They're declaring themselves the peers of God," he says. "In other words, they are not the sons of God. They are the sons of man. Does that make sense?"

"Pretty much," I say.

Louise is off gathering information for a divorce case, so I sit around alone and read most of the afternoon, stopping only to feed the cats and myself. The daylight drains from the sky. By the time she gets home, it's late enough that we start getting ready for bed.

After I brush my teeth and rinse my mouth with various blue liquids, I join her in the bed. The light goes out, and the dark surrounds us. I tell her about the info I pumped out of Randy.

"What do you think?" I say.

"I think the old guy is loony," Louise says. "You really think he set himself on fire?"

"I don't know. They wanted that book badly enough to trash this place," I say. "Who knows what they're thinking?"

"Loony or not, Randy makes one good point, though," she says. "We should be following those two disciples of Farber's."

"You think so?" I say.

She nods in a way that reminds me of kindergartner.

"Think about it," she says. "Whether Farber set himself on fire or not, those are the guys most likely to know something. I doubt they'd talk to us, but we could tail them."

"Would we really learn anything just following them around?" I say.

She rolls her eyes.

"Following people around is about 80% of my job," she says. "We can learn plenty."

"Alright," I say. "I guess you're the expert."

"There's not much to it," she says. "Keep your distance. Observe and don't be observed. That's about it."

"Pretty straight forward," I say.

"Still, you're a noob," she says. "I should follow the psycho and you should follow the wimpy one."

"Not a chance," I say.

"You said that everyone is scared to death of Cromwell, yeah? I've heard some of the stories," she says. "Well, what if he spots you? I've been at this a long time, I know he won't see me."

I kind of want to ask her about the stories, since I've yet to actually hear any of the specifics. But I feel that would weaken my position, so I skip it.

"I'm following Cromwell," I say. "I know how to handle these people."

She gives me a long look.

"Fine," she says.

- 14 -

I stand in the foyer of an apartment complex across the street from Cromwell's, watching his place through the window in the front door. So far, there are no signs of him.

This hallway smells like clam chowder, New England style, which reminds me of the Thai soup as well as Will's impassioned speech about his right to eat shellfish a few days ago. It also reminds me of the puffs of kinked hair sprouting from his ears.

Time drips by in slow motion, and Cromwell remains out of sight. Every few minutes, someone comes out of their apartment to get their mail or leave the building. They give me dirty looks as they enter the foyer and spot me, so I glare at them. I find glaring gets people to leave you alone most of the time. I bet if I tried to play it all incognito, someone would have confronted me by now about why I'm standing in their apartment building. By behaving aggressively, I put them on the defensive. They decide the confrontation would be too risky. It's sort of like how they say if you try to rip a shark's eye out during a shark attack, it will leave you alone. It's just looking for food. It doesn't want to risk permanent damage.

Or maybe I'm just really bored, and it's more entertaining to glare. For example, I decided an even better way to get people to leave me alone would be to say hi to them while scratching my dick for an uncomfortably long interval. Only a man bored to the point of despair would conjure an idea like that.

Someone finally exits Cromwell's building, but it's not him. It's a lady with sunglass and a scarf over her hair. She looks like she's from a different era, like a Jackie Onassis type. She walks slowly with her head down. One hand pins the scarf to the crown of her head like the wind might blow it away.

Is this the walk of shame? It could be. It could very well be.

You know what? Now that I think about it again, I want to revise my prior statement. It definitely smells like Manhattan style clam chowder in this hallway. Not sure what I was thinking when I said New England style earlier. Frankly, that couldn't be further from the truth.

After about six years pass (very slight exaggeration), Cromwell finally pushes through the front door of his building. My spine straightens to attention like a dog spotting a squirrel through the window. I almost want to press my face to the glass and bark maniacally at him, but instead I just watch as the target of my stakeout saunters down the avenue.

He's one of those short guys that seem excessively wide without being fat. His hair is black and has a lot of volume to it, particularly for a man. It's a side part with a pompadour-ish puff to it that bounces with every step. Actually, it might be more accurate to say that it flops rather than bounces.

I let him get some distance on me and slip out of the foyer, leaving the chowder smell behind for the smell of the city, which I'm sure will be just as pleasant.

We move through the streets, me trailing by about a half of a block. I track him by the flop of black hair and the bobbing navy blue hoodie. We pass the bums hanging out in front of McDonald's and take a right on Ninth Street. That's the first prominent smell– McDonald's fries. Not so bad after all.

Cromwell stops at a hot dog stand, so I guess this guy is some kind of health freak. After waiting in line, he acquires a meat tube I can't identify from my vantage point, but I'll take a guess and say he went with the bratwurst.

He mills around eating it, so I have to mirror his milling around at a distance. I pretend to tie my shoe for a long time. A lady with a kind face looks like she's about to offer me some help with it, probably assuming I have a number of problems, but I shake my head at her and she lays off. Really thankful I didn't have to resort to the dick scratching thing here, because she seems like a genuinely sweet lady.

Cromwell moves on, and I follow suit. We walk for a long while this time, making a right here and a left there. Block after block of chain stores and restaurants slide by on the sides of the road.

We climb a hill. The view from the top looks down on a swarming mass of humanity. I'm not sure what's going on. It appears to be a park with maybe a couple of rows of booths set up. The crowd undulates around the booths. From this distance it seems more like one entity that moves like choppy water rather than a bunch of individuals.

As I get closer, I pass a man toting a plastic bag full of corn on the cob, and it clicks. It's a farmer's market. I can't help but wonder how many people ate a bratwurst on their way to get a bunch of organic lacinato kale today.

Suddenly, I don't see him. No flop of hair. No navy blue hoodie. I pick up the pace a little, scanning the sidewalk in front of me again and again.

A tall guy wearing a beanie takes a quick right, and the flop of hair swings back into view. No worries. He was just screened from my vision. Still, I close the gap quite a bit. He'll be a lot tougher to stick with in this crowd, so I'll have to take some chances.

We stride onto the walkway that runs past the booths, and now we're completely engulfed by human bodies. Cromwell takes high steps and twists his shoulders and contorts himself to pick his way through the crowd. He looks like a salmon fighting his way upstream.

I lose him for a split second and then find him again, stopped at a fruit vendor. He picks up peaches from a bucket one at a time, pressing each of them with his thumb before putting them back. He gets out his wallet and hands the farmer some money. The vendor dumps a little bucket of peaches into a bag and hands them over.

With that, we're moving again. He stops to look over some eggplant and asparagus but gets going within seconds. He isn't so quick at a booth with a ton of greens – spinach, kale, collards, chard. Cromwell feels up every leaf in the place. I'm waiting for him to start shoving dollar bills down into the little band that holds the bunches of green together.

He purchases a variety of the leafy stuff. After paying, he turns, and he's gone. Just like that, he disappears into the crowd. I stand on my tiptoes to no avail. I dart between people in the direction that seemed to make the most sense as his likely trajectory, but I find no trace of the guy.

Changing gears, I turn around and hustle out of the booth area, thinking that so long as I beat him to the exit, he'll eventually have to come out. If I wait at this bottleneck I should be able to catch him and resume following.

I lean on a lamp post and watch the people file in and out of the market, all walks of life. I hold my phone in my palm in front of me and pretend it's a smart phone I can use to do awesome stuff instead of a 2004 shitty phone I really need to upgrade as soon as possible. I figure from a distance, it's at least a plausible thing for a guy to be doing while leaned up against a lamp post without drawing attention. Onlookers can't see that this is practically a rotary phone I'm holding.

Rows of endless people stream into the market with nothing and exit with produce. I guess, technically, many walk in with empty reusable cloth grocery bags and walk away with said bags filled to the brim with organic fruits and veggies. None of them are the guy I'm looking for, in any case, so it's not of much use.

I wait. I pretend to swipe the touch screen that doesn't exist on my phone. I chuckle at the imaginary text I just received and piston my thumbs in a fake reply.

Cromwell doesn't show. It's like he crawled into a display of potatoes and hunkered down to wait me out. I feel like a fool.

So my first following session was a bust. Louise is going to be disappointed. She always thinks I'm going to be great at everything.

I turn around and Cromwell is standing about three feet from me, sucking a grass green drink through a straw and looking right at me. He looks bored.

"Hey, Grobnagger," he says, easing the drink away from his mouth. "You tried one of these smoothies?"

I hate how everybody knows who I am.

"No," I say.

"Why you following me, bro?" he says.

"Seems like you're the one following me," I say.

"Nah. You followed me for like six blocks," he says. "Watched me eat a bratwurst and everything."

I knew it! I knew he'd go for the bratwurst.

"How was that?" I say.

"The bratwurst?" he says. "It was baller as hell, bro. It was a beer brat. That's the way to go, I think. I ain't down with any of that cheese stuffed crap."

Baller? So he's one of those.

"Yeah, that's cool," I say.

He squints at me, so I squint back at him. I'm not sure why I'm so quick to antagonize people of late, but it's kind of fun.

"You still have them seizures or what?" he says.

"It's been a while," I say.

He laughs a little, the wrinkles around his eyes relaxing.

"I can only imagine the shit you've seen, Grobnagger," he says. "From the way people talked, I kind of figured you'd be all stuck up and what not, but nah. You ain't like that at all."

"From the way people talked, I thought you'd be a lot more psychotic and a lot less drinking a green smoothie right now," I say.

Upon being reminded, he takes a big drink and then points at the cup.

"This shit is bomb, dude," he says. "It keeps me feeling up."

"So now what?" I say.

"What do you mean?" he says.

"Well, I was following you. Now you know about it," I say. "So what do we do now?"

He squints again and sucks down the last of his drink, the straw doing that annoying puttering noise when it runs out of fluid.

"Are you hungry?" he says.

I don't have to think about this long.

"Well, yeah," I say.

- 15 -

As we stride through the doorway of Cromwell's apartment building, part of me wonders if this is a terrible idea. I'm voluntarily walking into the home of the enemy. I guess playing all of that poker, I've learned to trust my read on people, though. This guy doesn't seem like a threat at all. A little dim, maybe? Sure.

Plus, he said, point blank, that he has food. Sounds pretty legit to me.

We walk up two flights of stairs and bank left into a hallway, stopping outside of apartment 336. A piece of wood stands between us and this weirdo's apartment. I'm given one last chance to turn back as he digs out his keys. I search my feelings and find no urge to flee the scene, though.

"I think you're going to like this, Grobnagger," he says as he twists the key and opens the door.

I'm not sure what to make of this statement, but it all comes clear as I cross the threshold into his place. The first thing my eyes are drawn to: a mural on the far wall depicting what looks like a mish mash of tarot imagery. In the dead center and largest of all, a winged, horned demon perches on an altar with his weird bird feet. He's fat and red with a stark white face and a black beard. He holds a flaming torch in his left hand, and a pentagram gleams above his head.

Below him a naked man and woman are shackled in chains that lash them to the beast's altar. Looking closer, though, they are not a normal man and woman after all. Small tails and horns sprout from their bodies as well.

A yellow sun gives off jagged, triangular light in the upper left. Another demon sits on a rock pile below the sun, playing a violin. This demon's skin gleams gray, and he looks more slender than his brethren. Something about his demeanor and facial expression suggests that his fiddle playing style would be best described as "shredding."

Elsewhere in the room, two coffins lean up against the walls as decorative flourishes. Black flags serve as curtains. Macabre carvings and sculptures line the shelves and tabletops.

All together, the interior design looks like something out of the Satanist issue of Martha Stewart Living or possibly the set of an Ozzy Osbourne music video circa 1983. I could see Randy Rhoads standing up on the arm of this couch with his legs about double shoulder width apart, playing a sweet solo with that devil mural behind him.

"What do you think?" Cromwell says after a while.

"It looks awesome," I say. "Good luck getting your security deposit back, though."

He laughs.

"I didn't show you the best part yet," he says.

He leads me over to one of the coffins and opens it. A crushed velvet looking material lines the inside, looks pretty normal. He grabs the velvet and pushes it to the side, though, revealing that this coffin is covering a doorway.

"What?" I say.

He smiles like he's in a Crest commercial and does one of

those hiss laughs through his teeth. The sound sort of reminds me of a cat puking. His face glows, though. I think people have won the Nobel Peace Prize and been less proud than this.

"Go 'head," he says, gesturing to the doorway.

Please don't be a sex dungeon. Please don't be a sex dungeon.

I step through the casket, and my eyes adjust to the dimness in this hidden chamber.

Great.

It's a sex dungeon.

Just kidding.

The wood floor in this room is sparse. A black table cloth drapes a small piece of furniture in the center of the room. Atop its surface, I spot a dagger, a fake skull, a cup and what looks to be a few bundles of herbs and spices.

The rest of the room is pretty barren. A couple of wooden chairs sit near the table, but the rest is exposed wood floors and blank white walls. It's quite sparse compared to the Satanist's wet dream that is the living room.

"This is my altar room," he says.

Not sure what to say, so I say:

"Nice."

"Yeah, I like to keep this a little more low key," he says. "The living room out there is for show, but this?"

He stretches out his arm, gesturing around the room.

"I don't need all of that glitz in here, bro," he says. "Nah. That kind of tinsel would only distract my focus. I figure you know what it's like, though. Shit, I don't need to tell Jeff Grobnagger about all this."

I nod, but I have no idea what he's talking about. And

frankly I'm starting to get a little upset.

I was told there would be food.

When Cromwell invited me over for food, I never would have guessed it'd be spaghetti, but here we are. It has come to this. He plops noodles out of a strainer and into a sauce pan full of simmering red marinara. Then he flips the pasta around with some tongs. He lifts the pan and dishes a serving of spaghetti onto a black plate and places it in front of me.

"I ain't braggin'," he says. "But I make a killer marinara."

Steam rises from the plate, coiling toward my face. It smells pretty good – a tomato aroma that has some foreign notes. He swivels away from me and twists back to grind aged Parmesan cheese onto the noodles.

"There," he says. "Now keep in mind, this is a frozen version of my sauce. Still killer as hell, for sure, but it's massively baller when it's fresh, bro. Massively."

Baller.

Again.

Massively so, for good measure.

I take a bite. It's quite acidic but also a nice balance of sweet and tart. The flavor grows more complex as it unfurls on my palate. It's a pure tomato flavor, not shrouded by spices or anything like that, but seasoned to enhance the actual tomato taste into something unbelievably delicious, somehow bold and subtle at the same time. I realize that if tomatoes tasted like this off of the vine, I would eat them like apples.

"Well?" he says, watching me chew.

"Baller," I say, shaking my head. "Massively, massively baller."

He smiles and nods. Now that the reviews are in, he plates himself a smaller serving and takes a seat across from me.

"Druzba tomatoes," he says. "That's my secret. They don't sell them at the super market or anything, so most people have no clue how delicious they are. They don't pick the produce varieties at the store based on flavor. They pick them based on looks and durability."

We eat.

As I finish up, I realize this might be a good time to ask some questions.

"So all of the League people say you're a crazy freak that wants to drink baby's blood and stuff," I say.

He laughs.

"They're just scared of the League dying off," he says. "The way I see it, the League has run its course. If it ever served a purpose, as a gateway to get people into this kind of stuff or what have you, that is past. It's a dog and pony show now. A club for people with quirky tastes and not much more. Solely superficial in practice – the little meetings and whatever. I've always wanted for our group to split off and be more serious. No baby's blood or nothing stupid like that, but I thought we could just be serious students of the arcane, right?"

I nod.

"Farber never wanted that, though," he says. "He said the League is an institution with some history, some tradition, and those things have power. Why throw that away, when we can bend the organization to our will and utilize its strengths? He was always more political than me, though."

"So what was the deal with Farber, anyway?" I say. "Why'd he kidnap me?"

Cromwell chews, swallows, looks at me.

"He didn't like to divulge the details of his plans. Even to the people closest to him," he says. "But I can tell you this. Everything he did, he did for power. I'm sure he thought you were a way to get power. Beyond that, I don't really know."

He shrugs.

"I don't get it," I say.

"Well, think about it this way," he says. "People believe in you. Your seizures and dreams and all of that? They believe in it. That gives you power right there. To Farber, belief was like a currency. It was energy that he felt could be spent. All of those illusions he did at the diner? Just a way to make people believe."

"So those were just illusions?" I say.

He smiles.

"I think so," he says. "Riston would never tell me how he did any of it, so I was torn. On one hand, if he had that kind of power, he'd probably use it for something bigger. On the other, I always thought he was too lazy to practice enough to get that good at sleight of hand."

He slurps down the last of his pasta.

"I guess anything is possible," he says.

"Do you think he set himself on fire?" I say.

"No," he says. "He was the type of guy to never be out of control. Never got drunk or anything. Never really loosened up, even in private. I can't see him taking a risk like that. He'd find a way to be sure before he pulled the trigger."

"I'm going to level with you. He doesn't exactly sound like a barrel of laughs," I say.

A lone puff of laughter exits Cromwell's nostrils.

"For real," he says. "He could be a total dick. He was an interesting cat, though. He knew how to do so many things, and when you hung out with him, you felt like epic events were always just around the corner."

"So if he didn't torch himself," I say. "Who did it?"

"I couldn't tell you," he says. "I mean, I've thought about that at length, and I've got nothing. No hunches. Not a single guess. It makes no sense to me."

He rises and moves to the sink to rinse our plates.

"Can I ask you something?" he says.

"Sure," I say.

"Were you scared?" he says. "When you had those seizures and went wherever the hell you went, you know? Was it scary?"

"In a way, yeah," I say. "But then I wasn't as scared as it seems like I should have been. It was hard to think straight sometimes."

"I get that," he says. "Man, I wish I could see it for myself."

I walk in the dusk, the sky going ashy around me. Apart from me, the streets are just about void of pedestrians now, nothing like when I followed Cromwell to the farmer's market earlier. The bustle died off, and the city feels lonely again, stark and gray and harsh. That's how I know it best.

It's getting chilly, so I zip my hoodie up all the way. It helps a little.

I'm not sure what to feel at this point. I'm a little confused, I guess. Everybody told me over and over again how scary Cromwell was. I was basically expecting him to be a werewolf wielding a chainsaw, but it was nothing like that. He just seemed like a regular guy with exceptionally bad taste in home decor. I'm starting to think that these cult people are all too imaginative for their own good. They see a monster in every shadow.

I go back over the things he said about Farber. He seemed pretty genuine about all of it, but he sure didn't seem very upset. I've known people that got choked up about a dead dog 15 years later. I'm not saying he needed to squirt out some tears or anything so dramatic. He just seemed unfazed entirely, and something about it felt off.

Whether that means anything important is another debate all together, of course. Maybe he's just not so in touch with his emotions. I find there's a direct correlation between a human being's sensitivity and the frequency of their usage of the word "bro." If you say bro more than 50 times a day, for example, I think you're clinically considered a sociopath. Use over 100 bros? Now you're a psychosexual sadist. Fact.

Either way, maybe Louise's hunch was right. She said there was no way Farber lit himself up, and Cromwell said the same.

I wait at an intersection, and the wind from the cars rushing past saps the warmth from my face until my cheeks sting. For a split second I consider clenching everything up to make the world turn warm and white, but it doesn't seem right somehow.

The light changes, and I cross the street. The cold crawls down my face to spread over the rest of me. I shove my hands deeper in my hoodie pockets, but it doesn't seem to help much.

I wonder where Glenn is right now. Is he OK? What about Amity? Will we ever cross paths again? I hope she's safe, either way.

I see the hot dog vendor pushing his cart on the other side

of the street. I guess he's done for the night. And then the stalking mission flashes through my head in fast speed – watching Cromwell's building from the foyer, following him, and ultimately eating a meal with him.

It occurs to me suddenly that this never would have happened before. Back before all of the alley dreams and the time spent with Glenn and Babinaux and Louise, I never would have gone into someone's house like that and stayed pretty comfortable. I'd have stayed home. Even if I somehow wound up there, I would have been nervous and taken the first opportunity to get away.

All of this has changed not just my circumstances, but all of me. These experiences, they crept into my eyes and seeped into my pores and etched themselves into the wiring of my brain. They became a part of me, and the whole was changed.

I like that.

- 16 -

Babinaux sits in the living room once again. This time we drink vanilla chai with a touch of honey.

The conversation winds its way through the usual recap type stuff, and then we're quiet, sipping tea.

"So hey, whatever happened to your friend?" I say.

"Which one?" she says.

"The one you were telling me about," I say. "You said he was the saddest person you ever met."

She takes a deep breath before she answers.

"When he was 44, he killed himself," she says. "Hanged himself with one of those orange extension cords in his garage."

"Oh," I say. "Wow, I'm sorry."

"It was very sad, but it was a while back," she says. "We weren't very close by that time."

We're quiet for a while. I can't help but feel really weird that this is the guy she compared me to.

"If you were ever feeling that down, you would tell me, wouldn't you?" she says. "Or you'd talk to someone about it, right?"

And this officially just got really uncomfortable.

"Yeah," I say. "I'm doing great, though. So, yeah."

"I know," she says. "I know."

Her words trail off into nothing. No sound. The silence squats on the room. It pins us to our seats and shifts all of its weight onto us, and the pressure builds and builds. We'll surely be crushed any second. Babinaux leaps into action, slaying the quiet with words:

"Listen," she says. "I came over to tell you that Randy wants you to do the water ritual tomorrow."

"OK," I say. "What's that? Like a baptism or something?"

"Kind of, yeah," she says. "It's not a big deal. You meditate in water for a bit."

"I can do that," I say. "Will there be a bunch of us like last time?"

"No," she says. "It's pretty rare. Only people that have shown an aptitude for this kind of thing do it."

"What do you mean by that?" I say.

"Things such as your dreams. It's an ancient rite of passage for potential shamans. It's supposed to clarify your spiritual thoughts and show you your path," she says. "Only a handful of our people have ever been deemed worthy, and it's been a while."

"Really?" I say. "How long?"

"Four years ago," she says. "Riston Farber did it."

"Oh," I say.

When I arrive at the old church, there's no sign that anyone is there. No lights in the windows. No cars in the lot. It's one of those small churches that probably had a congregation of about 40 at its absolute peak in 1956 or something. I look around the grounds for a minute, taking in the overgrown bushes lining the perimeter of the building and the pair of dead trees raising their rotten branches over the yard out back.

I walk back toward the front of the church. Weeds poke their way through the beds of gravel on each side of the doors, and the blades of tall grass sway in the breeze and hiss as they brush against each other.

Whenever the wind dies down, it's quiet enough that I can hear the lights over the parking lot buzzing above me. I stand in the stillness just outside the door a moment longer, and a car engine growls somewhere in the distance.

I turn the knob, half expecting it to be locked, but the door swings free. It's dark inside, and it smells like old people, like all of the carpet and upholstery sucked up the elderly smell like a sponge for all of those years, and now it wafts the odor around whenever it gets someone alone in here. I feel around for a light switch and find one a few paces into the foyer. I flip it. Nothing happens. My fingers find another switch next to the first and try that. Still nothing.

The door slams behind me, and I jump at the sound, wheeling around in the blackness to brace myself for the attack from whoever slammed it. Panic grabs me by the throat. A quiver travels up my spine, my shoulders convulse, and my hands flail at the dark in front of me.

There's just enough light from the parking lot to see now that my eyes have adjusted a bit, though, and there's nothing there.

It was probably the wind or something.

I am dumb.

I take a deep breath, and as I exhale, a clatter arises somewhere in the building. It sounds muffled.

"Hello?" I say.

Nothing.

I shuffle a few steps further in, my arms stretched out in front of me, my fingers bouncing around like feelers on some creature from the bottom of the sea. Would this be a really weird time to start laughing? Because I feel the craziest smile on my face. It's making my cheeks ache.

My foot connects with something solid, and I totter forward. Now my arms shoot out to the sides to help me catch my balance. My torso lurches back and forth a couple times, but I remain upright.

Another clang and rattle. This time I can tell that it's coming from my left. I start moving that way, my feelers finding the smooth cinder block wall to the right to guide me. It's quite cool to the touch.

A few strides later, a glimmer of light becomes visible to my right. I look at it for a long time, trying to make sense of it. It's not enough to help me see much. The wedge of illumination comes from near the floor somehow, which I can't wrap my mind around. I tap my hands in that direction and find a doorway leading toward the glow, and a step beyond that, I feel some kind of handle or rail.

And with the shape of that metal railing, the answer pops into my head – a basement. It seems so obvious now, but it's a crazy feeling to look at something for a long time in the dark, unable to comprehend it.

I feel around some more, but I find no light switch in the vicinity. With quite a grip on the railing, I descend. I let my feet feel their way down, toeing up to the edge of every step and easing onto the next. It's slow going, yeah, but it beats death by staircase. They say that's one of the worst ways to go. OK, no one has ever said that, but still…

As I near the bottom of the steps, I peer deeper into the cellar, my eyes scanning the area for the source of light. There. It shines through a crack along the bottom of a door on the other side of the basement.

"Hello?" I say again, pausing on the steps.

Still nothing.

I press forward. My feet touch down on the basement floor, and I work my way toward the light, weaving around tiny chairs and a table that I assume are relics from some long forgotten Sunday school operation.

When I reach the door, I realize that I'm unsure how to proceed. Do I knock? Do I just barge in? I listen for a moment while I ponder my options. A series of squeaks and clicks emit from the other side of the door. I don't know why, but they sound harmless to me.

I twist the knob and push open the door, and the light spills onto me. Squinting, I see Randy fiddling with what looks like a giant washer or dryer partially set in the basement floor. The hatch on the front looks like it's made out of parts scavenged from an antique submarine or something ridiculous like that.

Randy throws open the door on the front of the tank. I expect to see a huge load of whites in there, but instead I see light dancing on the top of the tank, reflecting off of water. He pulls out a string with a pool thermometer on the end. Water drips off of it as he brings the thermometer to his nose and squints at it. It occurs to me that the dryer looking thing is about the length of a coffin, and for the first time in a while, I think I know where this is going.

I take a few steps into the room, and Randy senses my

presence, looks up and pops an ear bud out of his ear.

"You're late," he says, tossing the thermometer back into the water.

- 17 -

As I climb into the tank, it occurs to me that this would be a great prank to pull on someone else. I'm climbing into a tank that looks like a big dryer, completely naked, with a person I don't know that well manning the lid from the outside. And oh yeah, the handle on the inside? Broken.

Seems legit.

I bet I could kick my way out if I needed to, though.

I scoot into the tank, doing something like a crab walk until I'm all the way in and then stretching my legs out and leaning back on my elbows in a position somewhere between sitting and lying down. The water covers my legs and laps against my torso, one rivulet rushing over my chest. It's just warmer than lukewarm, sort of like bath water a couple minutes before you'd want to get out.

"Here," Randy says. "You don't want to get salt water in your ears. Trust me."

I turn, and he hands me some earplugs.

"So what do I do?" I say.

"You put them in your ears, genius," he says.

"No, I mean what do I do in here?" I say.

"Just lie back and relax," he says. He slaps the tank. "This thing will do the heavy lifting. After a time your brain flips over to theta brain waves. It puts you in a different state of mind, like meditating. It kind of opens the valve to your subconscious."

"That's it?" I say.

"Look, let's just say that anything that happens beyond that won't involve you trying," he says. "Just let yourself relax. It takes time to realize that you can trust the water. You won't sink."

I pinch the tips of the ear plugs and push them inside of my head. At first, it almost seems louder than before from the sound of the foam expanding to fill my ear canal. Right away there's a crackling noise that reminds me of adding milk to Rice Krispies, but as that is muffled, it sounds more like listening to the ocean in a shell.

I look back to give Randy a thumbs up or something, but he's already closing the door. The rectangle of light compresses into a tiny sliver, hesitating as he fumbles to latch the door, and then disappears all together.

The dark closes in on me, and the air seems to get thicker. I can't decide if that's my imagination or if the humidity in the tank actually causes that. Maybe it's a little of both. It's not exactly hard to breathe, but it's a little unpleasant.

I ease back into the water, letting myself float, though it's hard to do that all the way. I fight it a little. The water reacts to my motion, and I bob along with it. A little wave hits just right and a splash of warm salt water gets into the corner of my mouth.

Yum.

My neck is all tight. I try repositioning my limbs. It seems to help if I keep my feet shoulder width apart and my arms straight out to the sides. I hold still like that a while.

I try to let my mind wander away from the physical experience a bit, but it's hard to not consider all of the sensory information. My penis is significantly more buoyant than my sack, for example. Good to know.

Once the water settles and my bobbing ceases, I feel like I float a little higher on the water. With less of a risk of swallowing the water, I can really start to relax. I don't force it. I just let the muscles in my neck go first, and it spreads from there a little at a time. My calves and then thighs release their tension. Then it feels like the fiber in my biceps and triceps and deltoids uncoil.

I don't fight anymore. I just float. I lie awake in the dark, my eyes wide open. I realize that in a way this is nothing new for me. I spend a lot of time awake in the dark it seems, in bed at night looking at the warped reflections rippling in my imagination.

I have no idea if it's been five minutes or 30. I haven't moved in a long time, though, and I feel a calm building in me. It reminds me of a bubble expanding somehow. There's an element of anticipation to it, a sense of something forming and growing. Even so, it is without anxiety.

I'm so calm. It's like I'm floating inside and outside at the same time. The salt water forms a sea around me that helps me understand the sea within.

Pink shapes swirl in the air, stretching out to fill my field of vision. They kind of look like a multiplied version of what happens if you stare at a bare light bulb for too long except they seem to move with more purpose. I think they've been there a while, actually, and I didn't really notice them at first.

Now the pink swirls writhe around each other, somehow

more solid than before, like claymation tendrils braiding and coiling everywhere. It's not like I'm dreaming them. They exist physically, there in front of me, occupying space.

And then my arms and legs tingle, pin pricks advancing across my flesh, going wherever they like, and within seconds the tingle blossoms into an itch. This isn't like the pleasant itch in the white world. It packs some intensity. One part of me is tempted to scratch, but the majority says nay. It would break up the trance, so I'll have to ride it out.

Tangible objects begin to form among the pink tendrils now, but the tentacles cover them over so fast it's hard to see what's what. Watching it pries my mind away from the itching some, anyway.

And then I see the acoustic guitar I saved all of my paper route money for when I was 12. It's close enough to touch for a moment. But the fleshy pink cords wrap around it quickly, and for a second all I can see is the sound hole and the pick guard, and then it's erased entirely.

Next I see body parts tangle over each other. At first they look like mannequin arms and legs entwined and wriggling, but they're flesh. The wrists flick. The fingers twitch. But the tentacles usher them away as well.

And then I'm floating up and up and up, though I'm not really sure which way up is anymore. My body ascends, though. I can feel that. It just keeps going. Or maybe drift is the better word for it. It's slow, like the way a cloud moves.

Nothing is real anymore, not where I am. I'm just a shell in empty space, rising endlessly.

And I see my face in the tendrils, eyes closed, a warped version of myself like it's reflecting from the surface of swirling water. The eyelids flutter. The skin quivers. The tentacles surge and undulate about the face but do not touch it. It's me, but it's hollow. It's empty.

And I'm nauseous, and as I look upon the face the calm seeps away from me like the tide pulling away. And hatred and panic well inside of me. All the bad feelings that only find their way out in nightmares come out now. Shame opens in my mind. Guilt flowers. Doubt blooms. The dark touches the places that wither on contact, the places that I can't regulate or protect or understand, the injuries that need to be stitched up.

And the bubble bursts in my head, the insides gushing out like flood water overtaking a bridge.

And everything goes white.

- 18 -

Everything is bled white again, but I'm somewhere else. I lie
on a stripe of dirt etched into the grass – a path running
through a sparsely wooded area. The wind blows, and the
leaves whisper and hiss. So I can hear. I probe my ears with my
pinky fingers and find no earplugs. Interesting.

I'm still naked, though.

So that's good.

For a moment I lie still on the ground, watching the
branches sway in the breeze. If I try hard enough I can kind of
see through the wood. Everything is partially translucent,
myself included, which I realize as I hold my hand in front of
my face and look through it to watch the flit and flicker of the
leaves.

My hand falls to my chest, and I let the bliss wash over me.
No more hatred. No more panic. No more hollow face in the
tendrils. The white makes it all go away, and nothing can hurt
me. I feel whole – a universe all of my own that the outside
world cannot touch.

I stand. This patch of nature looks familiar, but I don't
know why. I don't think I've ever been here.

I stretch and feel a spiral of pleasure in the space between
every pair of vertebrae. I roll my neck, and the comfort touches
there as well. I take a deep breath, and my chest heaves.

There's little else to do, so I walk along the path. I don't get the sense that it leads to anything, but I follow it anyway. I don't really need to know where I'm going, I guess. I'm already here.

The trees reach gnarled limbs out over the walkway. In a couple of spots, I see branches from the opposite sides of the path crisscrossing each other in the air above me, and it looks like they're sword fighting. Or touching tips. Or both.

I walk for some time, though I have little sense of it in terms of minutes or hours. Step after step stretches back in my memory so far that it's hard to remember what came before the first one.

The ground about me seems to grow sandier as I move forward, and the trees grow smaller and more sparse. When the wind gusts little clouds of dust billow up like tiny smoke signals for no one. The sand squishes between my toes, all gritty and warm.

The sun heats the back of my neck. It's pleasant enough, though, and I note that I'm not sweating. I don't think I need any SPF here somehow.

The path leads me up a hill, my feet now sinking partially into sand with each step. I climb. As it gets steeper, I use my hands to help scale the peak, fingers clawing at the earth. There's little to grip, but I keep at it, fighting, ripping, scratching the ground. I earn every inch of progress.

I reach the summit, out of breath, little lines swirling at the corners of my field of vision. I feel the vein in the center my forehead throbbing, its meter erratic. When I picture it, it looks like a pulsing garden hose with skin draped over it. The throb evens out and then recedes, though. I pick the grains of sand out from under my fingernails while I regain my wind.

From the top of the hill, I can see a long way. The diminishing woods give way to desert before long, dunes rolling away into the distance. There's a fork in the trail up ahead, but the two paths seem to run in parallel, at least as far as I can see.

I jog down the hill. It's more like falling and catching myself over and over again than running. I'll give gravity the credit for the assist on this one. By the time I'm at the bottom of the hill, my knees are a little sore from the repeated shock absorption, but it's a sore that feels good - in the white world, at least - sort of like the itching. I sit for a moment and massage my knees just to focus on the ache. It feels so good, my eyelids half close and flutter, and my mouth waters.

And then I wake myself with the drool draining onto my leg from my nodded out head. I'm not sure how long I was out, but the sun sits higher in the sky. I wipe the saliva from my chin with the heel of my hand, and my fingertips brush the tip of my nose which is as cold as a bomb pop. It's weird because the rest of me is really warm.

I rise, ready to move forward, and so I do. The sand stings now as I trudge through it, crawling hot and dry up onto my feet with each step and reaching up for my ankles. I power through it.

I reach the split in the path and stop to think my options over, hands on my hips. The terrain to the right and left look about the same to me, just as they did from afar. I have no coin to flip, either. No reason to belabor the decision, though, I guess. For no particular reason, I choose the right handed path and get going again.

The sand sprawls to the horizon in front of me. One tiny sliver of me thinks walking into the desert nude is a terrible idea. The rest is down to do whatever.

I have to pick up my feet higher now because walking in the sand is so awkward. I feel like I'm marching, patrolling the dust, the decay. The stand stomp slows me down quite a bit, but I'm not that concerned. There's nowhere I'm really going anyway, right?

As I mount the first big dune, I feel the needle of fatigue in my legs for the first time. The soreness in my knee was one thing, this is another. The muscles clench up too hard, and I can feel it bite at every little fiber.

And for the first time I think about where the hell I really am. Suffering fatigue - something so human and ordinary and not at all of the white world I know - shakes my confidence a little. The white always soothes me, gives me faith that everything will be fine or already is, but this is no heaven. I'm walking into the desert – the place where the sun chars all, the place where the heat cooks the life out of everything.

And as if on cue, a black blur rises above the sand on the horizon. It bounces up and down and appears to shimmer in the heat haze vibrating off of the ground. A person, a human being dressed in black, walks on the other trail – the left handed path. I can't tell if they're walking toward me or away.

And then the blur descends, sinking out of my view. From my vantage point it looks like the person walked down a flight of stairs into a doorway in the sand, but they must be walking into a valley between dunes. The way they disappeared makes me think they're headed my way, but it's hard to be sure of anything out here with the heat distortion in all directions.

I speed up, trying to walk on the sides of my feet so I don't sink quite as deep. With urgency in my step for the first time, I cover a lot of territory in a hurry. The ground works at my flesh like an infinite supply of exfoliating beads, grinding away the outermost layer of skin.

I try to keep calm, to stay patient. But I can't. I can't.

And I'm running, sprinting, somehow willing my tired legs to push through the ache. I glide over the sand by sheer force of will.

The black shape rises from the horizon again, closer. Much closer. I see the face take shape as it pokes out from behind the dune, a familiar face.

It's Amity, plodding toward me, her face angled at the ground.

I freeze on the spot, going from full sprint to dead stop in 0.2 seconds.

And I want to yell and jump up and down and wave my arms, but I can't. I can't move. I have to concentrate to even make myself breathe.

And then her head pops up, and it tilts in my direction. She stops walking.

Does she recognize me?

"Hey," I manage to say.

Unfortunately I say it in a normal speaking volume that she couldn't possibly hear. Still, it's some progress.

She shields her eyes from the sun by cupping her hand at her brow. Her head juts out a bit. She's definitely looking right at me.

And then she turns and runs.

"Wait!" I yell.

And I'm sprinting again, sand flying out from under me. "Amity!" I say.

Why is she running from me? Did she recognize me?

And then I remember that the last time we met I kind of killed her. Plus, I'm naked. I look down to see a whole lot of shakin' goin' on. It really could be either of those things that set her on the path away from me, I guess.

So now I'm a naked guy chasing and yelling at a girl.

Pretty sweet.

I cross the sand between the paths on a diagonal, taking this trajectory to try to best erase the distance between us. I'm gaining on her.

Amity looks back over her shoulder at me, and her eyes get wide. I want to say something to her, something that might calm her. Instead I get the strangest feeling in my throat. I cough and a gush of water fills my mouth.

I stop running and cough again, and I feel the water enter my throat and the shock and revulsion as it touches the parts it's never supposed to touch. For a split second I can feel the burn of the sand on my feet, and the completely different burn in my wind pipe.

And then the desert vanishes, and I'm plunged into darkness.

Confused. Black nothing surrounds me. My eyes burn. I can't breathe. My limbs don't want to respond to my commands. I grit my teeth and will myself to not panic, and time goes into slow motion.

Think about what this could be. There must be some piece of information that can help me. I might only have a few seconds.

Salt.

I taste salt.

The saltwater.

I'm back in the tank, and I'm floating face down.

I try to reach out and push myself off of the bottom of the chamber, but my arm doesn't jolt into action so much as twitch a little, if even that. I twist my head to the right instead, pushing, pushing , rotating my shoulders to try to put as much of my weight as I can muster into it, and the momentum causes me to capsize.

I'm on my back again, head above water, but when I try to inhale, it doesn't work, like my chest is stuck. I turn my head, and my abdomen spasms. My diaphragm clenches so hard that my body arcs, and the liquid spurts out my mouth like it's spraying out of the jet on a hot tub. It pours out of me for what seems like so long, though perhaps the slow motion warps my perception, and then it pauses and starts again. After three bursts, the air gasps back into my lungs, all gurgle-y.

My lungs scald, and it feels like my mouth and nose are full of salty snot, but I can breathe. I listen to the repeating rhythm of the inhale and exhale, thankful to hear it.

Within a few minutes, my motor skills fade back in, a little dull but functional. I bang on what I guess to be the door to the tank.

I believe I'm done here.

- 19 -

I sit in a lawn chair, looking out at the courtyard bled white behind the church. A blanket drapes my shoulders, much of it dangling behind me like a cape. Randy set me up out here. He said it takes a while to reacclimate yourself to time and space after a long deprivation session, and it's common to sit somewhere peaceful a while and let it all come back to you.

My feelings vacillate between excitement and exhaustion, awe and fear. I crane my neck to stretch it, trying to get the balled up muscle to loosen its grip a bit.

I remember the events and images I just experienced in bits and pieces, like I can't have access to the whole all at once. Much of it is clouded around the edges, and I struggle to put the pieces in order. It's like trying to piece together the fragments of a dream. With every glimpse I do get, my belly twinges with equal parts butterflies and a fist clench of dread.

I see things when I close my eyes, pink tentacles and piles of sand stretching out into infinity, my warped face wavering as if on the surface of the sea. And Amity running from a naked man, of course. I picture myself – sprinting, red faced, yelling, dong flopping like crazy.

It seems funny in a way now, of course. More than anything, I'm glad to know she's still out there. That what happened back in the alley wasn't for keeps. It gives me hope that Glenn and I can find her at some point.

Where the hell is Glenn, anyway? I consider the notion that if I go back there, I may be able to find him as well. Maybe next time I can even wear some pants.

The wind blows in the courtyard, and the dead trees moan and creak. The door next to me swings open, and Randy leans out.

"You alright?" he says.

"Yeah," I say. "I think I'm ready to go."

He squints at me.

"How long do you think you've been out here?" he says.

"I don't know," I say. "Five minutes."

"Try 40 minutes," he says. "You should sit a while longer and let your brain get back to the Earth's physics."

"OK," I say.

He heads back inside. According to him I was only in the tank for 25 minutes before I started pounding on the door. He said typically people take about 40 minutes to reach a meditation like state and achieve the switch to theta brain waves – opening the valve to the subconscious as he called it. It makes me wonder how long I was actually having that experience. If it took me 20 minutes to get there, did everything else happen in five minutes? It seems impossible. It feels like I walked miles on that trail.

Of course, I'm certain that I saw Amity in the white world for real. Could it be a hallucination? Maybe it's possible, but I don't think so. It triggered the white world, which is still transpiring for me. It made it stronger while I was in the tank, though. I wasn't just looking through the white world. I was there.

Maybe it's just the eternal bliss affecting my brain, but I feel lucky to have seen and felt all of this tonight. If this exact stuff happens to anybody else, it's maybe a handful of people on the entire planet. Everybody else's imagination craves images and emotions like these so much, they line up around the block to go to the movies. I just close my eyes, and it's all there in front of me, lurching and swaying and writhing. Back on the beach, Duncan said there are others like me, but maybe their version is different from mine.

And I remember that there's one person I want to share it all with. I pull my phone out of my pocket and press the appropriate buttons. It goes to voice mail immediately, and I hear her voice encouraging me to leave a message. I never leave messages, though.

Oh well.

I hang up and shove my phone back into my pocket. I adjust in my seat, and the lawn chair squeaks under me.

All of my senses are heightened from my time isolated. The sounds and the smells out here take on such nuance, such richness of detail, that I feel like one of those wine tasters sensing every fruity and zingy and earthy note. I smell the way the grass scent mixes with the wet wood chips nearby. I hear with great clarity the scrape of dead leaves moving over the pavement on the other side of the lot.

These details calm me somehow. They make the part of me that's perpetually on the verge of despair from sheer boredom shut the hell up for once.

I know I won't be able to sleep tonight, though. I can feel the electricity flickering behind my eyeballs, a level of stimulation cranked well beyond the state of mind where sleep is possible. I can already picture myself, rolling around on the couch like a coked up werewolf, growling, snarling, grunting out weird phlegmy throat noises.

The door swings open again, and Randy leans out, thrusting something blue at me.

"Almost forgot about this," he says. "You need to stay hydrated."

It's a blue Gatorade. I take it.

"Thanks," I say.

I pop the top, and when I look back to say something to Randy, he's gone already. I wonder what he's doing in there. Maybe there's a kitchen, and he's baking some kind of strudel or something. Wait. Strudel or streusel? I can't remember.

I sip the blue drink. It detonates on my pallet – a bright, acidic punch laced with sweet and salt. The world about me jitters and fizzles around the edges. I feel my eyes drawn inward, crossing, and then the dizziness spirals into my head with such force that I grip the arms of the chair so it won't hurl me to the ground. I hold still, eyes narrowed to slits, knuckles gone whiter than white.

In time, the dizziness lets up, and the fizzle dulls away.

So yeah, I forgot about all of that. You really have to tread lightly with beverages in the white world. Sheesh.

I screw the cap back on the Gatorade and set it down on the grass next to the leg of the chair. I need to get stickers that say "high octane" or something to slap on all of my drinks from now on.

I pull the phone out and try again. Straight to voicemail. Louise's voice rings in my ear, but it's not real. It's empty. I hang up and cut it off.

It brings me down somehow, as down as you can be in the white world, anyway. I guess even bliss becomes meaningless if you're left alone. I take a deep breath and let it out slow.

No more of this.

I will myself to stop thinking, to let the swirl of words circle down the drain and be gone. I don't wonder. I don't ponder. I don't reason or reflect. I just sit.

I stare out at the dead trees, blank as hell.

When I get home, there's a note on the fridge that says:

"Sorry I've been so busy. Let's have lunch tomorrow.

-Louise"

And I feel a little dumb for getting so upset.

- 20 -

We sit at a picnic table, rotten wood coated with green lichen. Louise unzips a lunch satchel and pulls out a couple of sandwiches, peanut butter and jelly. Her hand sinks into the bag a second time, this time yanking free a sandwich baggie full of potato chips. She looks distracted, her eyes darting away from the food over and over.

I told her about most of the stuff that happened in the tank and the white world last night on the way over, but she didn't say much. I guess she's pretty obsessive about her work. Plus, she's remained pretty skeptical about what is happening to me. I get the impression that she thinks it's cute that I think any of it is real. I don't blame her, though. I probably wouldn't believe it either, if I were someone else.

I unwrap my sandwich and take a bite, following her gaze across the park to a man and woman sitting on a bench. This must be the perp and his mistress, up to no good. He's probably 60 with puffy white hair, sporting a damn turtleneck. It seems weird that someone is even willing to pay to document whatever infidelities this guy might be getting up to. Seriously, I struggle to fathom that someone's happiness hinges on Turtleneck's behavior.

Louise jots something in her notebook. She also has her camera at the ready, the gigantic lens partially shielded from sight by the lunch bag.

The first triangular half of my sandwich is gone, but she has yet to touch hers. I'm tearing into the chips pretty good, too. If she doesn't hurry, she may regret it. Then again, maybe she's not hungry. There's no evidence to suggest she is.

"I might need to go back at some point," I say. "To find Amity or Glenn. Or both."

Her eyes remain fixed on the bench beyond me. Without looking away she reaches for the camera, her hands moving with a steadiness I assume is to avoid drawing the notice a jerky motion might arise. She brings the camera to her eye, the off eyelid clinched tight. Her finger hovers over the button, ready to pull the trigger. After a long moment, she pulls it down and tucks it behind the bag again.

"False alarm," she says. "I thought that was going to be the money shot."

"Yeah," I say.

We're quiet for a moment. She finally takes a bite of the sandwich.

"Weren't you saying something?" she says.

"Yeah," I say. "I said I might need to go back to find Glenn and Amity."

"Back where?" she says.

"Back into the tank," I say.

"Dickhead!" she says. "You ate all of the chips."

"Yeah, sorry," I say. "I didn't think you were hungry, I guess."

Her eyes snap back to the bench, and the camera is in her hands in a flash. She adjusts the focus and snaps a few shots. I don't care to look, but I like to think that the lady pulled down the collar of the Turtleneck to give him a hickey.

"He put his arm around her," she says, snapping the lens cap back on. "Better than nothing."

I watch her eat a couple more bites of sandwich. Mine is long gone.

"I'm sorry," she says. "What were you saying, again?"

"I might need to go back in that tank," I say.

"What for?" she says.

I can't quite hide the agitation in my voice.

"To find Glenn and Amity," I say.

"Oh, right," she says. "Yeah, you should do that."

"It's kind of scary in a way," I say, but she's already locked onto the bench again, so I don't bother going on.

The Passat rolls down Park Street, whisking us in the general direction of home. Flecks of water flit against the windshield, so apparently our lunch in the park endeavor ended just in time. The rain taps out a steady rhythm on the windshield, and the sound calms me a bit, I think.

I try to tell myself that Louise is just busy. She carted me along while she worked so we could spend some time together since she's so swamped with cases right now. She's got a lot on her mind and all that.

But I can't help but feel rejected anyway. I get that when people don't listen to me, I guess. I don't know. Someone told me once that I have a habit of looking for rejection in all things.

Her phone buzzes from within her purse, and she digs it out and hands it to me.

"A text," she says. "Will you check it?"

I'm confused for a split second, but I guess it's because she's driving. I hate using other people's phones. Most of the time, I somehow press like 50 buttons on the touch screen accidentally as soon as the phone hits my hands, and then I'm panicking because the phone is calling someone saved in the contact list as "Mo-Mo," and I'm in no mood to explain all of this to Mo-Mo just now.

Anyway, that doesn't happen this time. I press a thingy and read the text.

"It's Dennis," I say. "He says, 'You gotta meet me ASAP. It's about your burn vic.'"

After a quick back and forth with Dennis, we change routes to meet him in the parking lot of a Marathon on West Street. I use the term quick loosely here, though. I had to type on the tiny keyboard, thumbs all atwitter. The worst.

We pull into the lot and park next to the police cruiser behind the building. Dennis gets out and strides over to the Passat. He wears a pair of wrap around Oakley's that remind me of Glenn and Mark McGwire.

"This is some crazy shit," he says en route.

He leans into the driver's side window of the Passat. He looks across the car and sees me. His face looks blank for a second, and then something registers.

"What up, Grobnagger?" he says, reaching through the vehicle to shake my hand.

"Hey," I say.

I never know if it's better to answer any variation of "What's up?" as though the person is literally asking what I'm up to or take it more as a general greeting and say hi. I feel dumb either way, so I guess there's no way to win this game. Whatever.

"So check this out. That burn vic, Farber?" he says "His body – POOF - vanished. It ain't at the morgue. It ain't nowhere."

"For real?" Louise says.

He smirks. I feel like Dennis is perpetually pleased with himself.

"How long do they keep bodies at the morgue?" I say.

"Someone's been watching some CSI. So the thing is, we hadn't officially identified him yet," he says. "Louise says word among the culties is that it's Farber, but officially, without cooperation from any of the League people, he's John Doe. He'd be at the morgue until we made a positive ID."

He spits on the ground.

"Anyhow, they want to keep that hushed up, so you didn't hear it from me," he says, moving back toward his car.

He stands in the open door for a second, one elbow leaned on the roof.

"Thing is, they keep that shit locked up, and that part of the building is under 24 hour supervision. Everybody through there has to sign in and out. So it's like some Houdini shit to get a stiff out of there," he says.

A drone of chatter blares from his walkie talkie. He presses the button and mumbles into it, rolling his eyes. Then he holsters the walkie talkie and turns back to us.

"I gotta go," he says.

He's in, slams the door, and the car is moving almost immediately. The cruiser rips out of the parking lot, Dennis gunning it to take the turn onto the street at top speed. He honks an obnoxious two note goodbye.

Dread bloats in my belly as we roll out of the Marathon parking lot. The absence of Farber's body bothers me, maybe even scares me a little.

Silence envelops the Passat's interior on the ride home. The tires slosh over the wet asphalt, but that's outside. Inside? Only quiet. Our thoughts tangle around us and keep our tongues still, I suppose, though I suspect the two of us are thinking about completely different things.

Louise probably wonders who, what, when and how someone got the body out of the morgue undetected, and where she can get said info to give to her client for an agreed upon sum. I'm wondering whether or not Riston Farber has risen from the dead. If so, is he stomping around all burned up? Like a burnt chicken skin version of the crypt keeper or something? I can't really imagine that frail piece of extra crispy walking the Earth.

The prospect scares me, nonetheless. I picture the fear in Randy's eyes when he talked about the notion of someone using the book to come back, the power it would bestow upon them. I believe he said that if it happened, we'd be up shit creek. And immediately the image resurfaces of me brandishing a turd paddle, fighting my way upstream.

Louise puts on the turn signal, and the click clack breaks the spell of the silence, erasing all turds from my mind. We both seem able to move again, and we look at each other.

"We need a plan," Louise says.

"I know," I say.

I bet Glenn would have a kickass plan at the ready. And probably a thermos of chamomile tea, too, to calm our nerves.

"You should talk to Cromwell again, and I'll talk to Stan,"

she says. "Don't tip off that you know about the body, at least not right away."

"Yeah, I get it," I say.

She thinks I might be able to tease something out of him or trip him up if I play it right. Let's get real, though. In a best case scenario, I might tease out a free meal.

Not that I'm knocking that. I mean, I could eat.

- 21 -

I stand on the doorstep of Cromwell's building, my fingertip still lingering on the button next to the scrawl of his name. A buzz sounds from somewhere inside, and the door pops open. I grab it and pry it wide, finding it surprisingly heavy.

I climb the steps, passing a lady with crazy eyes on the way up. She smiles at me, but with her eyes open that wide, it looks more like an animal baring its teeth as a warning.

When I get to apartment 336, the door is opened a crack. I assume Cromwell left it open as an invitation for me to come in, but I hesitate anyway. What if burned up zombie Farber is in there, hovering spoons to force throw at my face?

I move through the doorway, passing through the entry hallway into the living room. No charred zombies here. Cromwell sits on the couch with a bag of pretzels in his lap. His eyes are so glued to the TV that he doesn't notice my presence. There's something funny about a person snacking and watching TV in front of that devil mural. I picture his mom fixing him a snack, "Now, who wants demon pretzels and bug juice?"

"Hell yeah!" he says, raising a fist full of pretzels in the air.

I glance at the screen. Football.

"Oh, hey Grobnagger," he says. "What up?"

"Hey," I say.

He looks at me for a second.

"So what's up?" he says, and there's an edge to his voice this time.

Goddamn it! I guess he meant the question literally and not as a greeting, and now he's annoyed that I didn't answer it. See? You cannot win this game.

"Nothing much," I say. "I was just in the neighborhood."

He squints and tosses a couple of pretzels in his mouth.

"That's cool," he says, between crunches. "I'm just watching the game."

He raises a hand clutching pretzels, which I guess is a gesture to the TV.

"I see that," I say.

"Well, have a seat," he says.

I do this, plopping onto the loveseat perpendicular to the couch.

"You watch sports?" he says.

"A little," I say.

He chews with his mouth open.

"Seems like most people either watch a lot or none," he says.

"Well, I watch a little," I say. "I guess it puts me in the minority, but I can get some entertainment out of it without painting my face and starting a blog."

He chuckles, but the laugh dies in his throat, and he's yelling at the TV, flecks of food spraying from his mouth. I look up to see players scrambling for a loose ball on TV.

"Unreal," he says, leaning back. "Second turnover already, and it ain't even halftime."

He watches with such rapt fervor, I don't feel there's a good opening to ask him anything Farber related. I decide to table it until the game reaches the half.

We watch for a while. The announcers spout clichés and mock outrage and feigned excitement. One guy implores the audience to "hold on to your hat" four times in a 10 minute segment. Meanwhile, Cromwell strings together obscenities and hurls them at the screen. Many of the combinations make little sense, which makes them more interesting.

During the next commercial break, he points the open end of the bag of pretzels at me and gives it a shake. I take a few. Not bad, but I could really use that bug juice to wash them down.

Seriously, pretzels without a beverage? Lunacy.

Cromwell must sense my ire. He runs out of the room during a booth review and comes back with a pair of beers. He uses a lighter from the coffee table to pop the lids off and hands me one without even looking at me.

"His left foot was out of bounds," he says, pointing at the screen. There's a sense of pleading in his tone.

I examine the bottle in my hand. It's Sam Adams. I take a sip. It's been a long time since I drank a beer, so I can feel my lips pull down a touch at the corners due to the bitterness. It's not bad, though. Out of the mass marketed beers, I think this is among the best. There's almost a spiced flavor in there somewhere.

To Cromwell's disappointment, the play stands as called. The game gets back underway. In the distraction, my old habits kick in, I guess, and a couple slugs later, I've chugged the beer down. I set the empty bottle on the table.

"Damn, Grobnagger," he says.

"I was thirsty," I say.

"If I knew you were going to pound 'em down like that, I would have brought you more than one," he says.

He runs to the kitchen to grab a couple more and sets both of them by me. This time he remembers a bottle opener, too. I didn't know I was signing on for this. I consider nursing the next one, but then I figure screw it. It's almost halftime now. Maybe the beers will lubricate my brain and help me come up with an angle of approach in my interrogation.

Alcohol slows other people down, but it doesn't seem to do that for me. It just relaxes me, makes it easier to talk to people, dulls the outside world a bit. My mind stays sharp, at least until I drink enough that I can't walk.

I pour 24 ounces of Sam Adams down the old drain between the two minute warning and halftime. Cromwell seems impressed by this.

"I didn't know you partied like this, man," he says.

"Can I ask you something?" I say. "Did you ever think Farber would figure out how to do it?"

"Do what?" he says.

"Come back from the dead," I say. "I mean, you talk about being a serious student of the arcane, but you also talk about Farber like he's a con man, more or less. I was just wondering if you believed in him or not."

"That's a good question," he says. "It's hard to say, bro. I mean, faith is a choice, right? I choose to believe that there's more going on in the universe than the physical realm that we perceive. It makes some sense to me intuitively, and I want to believe that. I look for ways to connect to it or experience it or verify it or whatever the shit you want to call it, and I do that both internally and externally. But it's not like I believe it entirely on a conscious level. Like say you ask me that question about Farber resurrecting, and part of me thinks 'Of course not. It's ridiculous.' But the part of me that wants to believe and pursue all of this occult stuff still believes it to be possible. That's why I put my time into it. To me, that's what faith is. It's the choice. It has nothing to do with believing all of it absolutely. Like the beliefs people inherit from their parents without putting any thought into it? That's not faith to me."

OK.

What the hell?

That was well put. This guy might be singlehandedly disproving my theory about the correlation between the usage of the term "bro" and IQ or sensitivity or whatever. Or perhaps he's the exception that proves the rule.

"Well said," I say.

I think for a second.

"So did he talk about resurrection a lot?" I say.

"It came up," he says. "He talked about a lot of shit, though. If I had to sum up his point of view, I'd say he often brought things back to the realm of control. He was always talking about using the things he learned and acquired to gain power, to use them to achieve something in the physical world. I was probably always more philosophical and shit in my approach. I just want to connect to something outside of myself, you know? He didn't seem as interested in that part of things. That was his flaw, I think, and maybe it's what did him in."

He slaps the wall behind him.

"That mural?" he says. "That's what it means. People think

it represents pure evil or some nonsense. In the tarot, the devil is the symbol for obsession with the physical realm. His chains shackle the two people here, right? When they throw away their spiritual desires in favor of dedicating their passions and thoughts and hearts to money and sex and their careers and so on, they do as the devil pleases, they chain themselves to his altar. I wanted it up there to remind me of what I really care about and what I don't."

He scratches his chin.

"Oh, shit. You already finished both of those?" he says, pointing at the empties on the coffee table.

"Yeah, I'm probably good, though," I say.

"Nah," he says. "Game's only half over."

He hustles out of the room and returns with more beer. This time it's tall boys that are blends of Bud Light and Clamato called Chelada.

"What the hell is this?" I say.

"Just try it," he says. "It's delicious."

I open the can. It smells like tomato juice with a little bit of beer. I taste it. It tastes like tomato juice with a little bit of beer. There is also a salty punch, a clam flavor and a hint of something like lime.

"Well?" he says.

"Not bad," I say. "If I'm ever in the mood for beer mixed with tomato juice mixed with clam juice mixed with lime, I'll know what my go to beverage is, that's for sure."

He chuckles.

"So let's say a burned up Farber zombie walked through that door right now," I say. "What would you do?"

His eyes tilt toward the ceiling as he imagines this scenario.

"I'd chop its head off with that katana blade leaned up against the coffin over there," he says. "And then I'd probably go change my pants."

I laugh.

"Well, he's bound to turn up somewhere," I say.

His face looks blank, and then his brow crinkles.

"What do you mean?" he says.

"You know," I say. "About the body."

He doesn't move. He just stares at me.

"I think I don't," he says.

"Oh," I say. "Farber's corpse? It went missing from the morgue. I figured you already knew."

"No way!" he says, sitting forward.

On TV, a running back breaks off an 86 yard run for a touchdown, but Cromwell barely notices. His eyes don't waver from me.

"Yep," I say.

"Unbelievable," he says. "Do the cops know what happened?"

"I think they know something," I say.

I pause here under the guise of taking a drink, but really I just want to watch his reaction.

"But they're playing it close to the vest for now," I say.

"That's... Wow," he says. "Wow."

He sits back in his seat and takes a long slurp from his can.

With the sun gone, the city chills down to the point that I can see my breath hover in the air. I'm thankful for those beers after all. The drunk keeps me warm on the walk home from Cromwell's. Even without a jacket, the heat radiates out from my torso like my insides are a cranked up furnace.

I feel reasonably confident that Cromwell had nothing to do with the disappearance of Farber's corpse. Unless he's an Oscar caliber actor, which I doubt, that's the story his words and demeanor tell me. Anything is possible, yes, but I trust my instincts. I trust my feelings.

I step over a pothole filled with sludgy water as I cross the street, and it reminds me of the alley. It seems like all of that happened years ago now. It's weird how time winds you on a path away from every event in your life until it feels cold and distant.

I replay some of Cromwell's answers in my imagination as I shuffle down the sidewalk. When I said the police knew something, he showed no signs of alarm. He looked pretty much ecstatic from the moment I mentioned the disappearance, in fact. I also felt like he was a little dismissive of Farber's motives and ideas in a way that suggested little chance of collusion. His comments also didn't seem like the kind of remarks you'd make about someone you recently killed.

That seems to rule out most of the angles I could see for him being involved.

Then again, maybe I should have been more direct. Perhaps I should have asked him point blank about the morgue toward the end there. I don't know. I'm not some interrogation expert.

As the blocks pass by, the cold crawls up my arms and legs to do battle with the furnace in my abdomen. I'm not far from home now, though. Soon, I'll be with Louise, and we'll be warm, and none of this will matter for a little while.

- 22 -

I dig through Glenn's fridge. I've put a pretty big dent on the local food supply, so all that's left is a six pack of beer, condiments, a jar of homemade pickles, a package of frozen dinner rolls along with a bunch of random stuff in Tupperware containers in the freezer. It appears to be tomato based liquids for the most part - like soup or sauce, most likely. Hard to tell for sure in a solid state.

At some point I'm going to need to go buy groceries, I guess, which I dread. He kept the place stocked pretty well, but I've eaten like a king for a few weeks now.

Sitting at the snack bar, I wrench open the pickle jar, scissor a pickle spear between two fingers and take a bite. It crunches nicely. The vinegar is bright, the garlic robust, and the jalapeno bites at the back of my throat. In other words, it's effing delicious.

I try to call Louise again, and it goes to voicemail immediately. Yep. I fight the urge to throw the phone through the wall. When that swell of rage passes, I get the impulse to shatter the pickle jar, which I meet halfway by savagely eating another pickle from it, tearing, gnawing, grinding it into mush.

Pretty convenient that she stops answering my calls now that she gets what she wants, isn't it? I join the League and start following all of her orders, and she vanishes into a puff of smoke more and more frequently.

I pull the rolls I found in the freezer out of the oven and slather peanut butter all over them, scraping it out of the bottom of the jar. Open faced sandwiches. A goddamn delight.

Even as good as the food tastes, eating is supposed to be satisfying, and I find no contentment in this meal. I just grow angrier and angrier. It'd be nice to talk to someone about the stuff that's going on, namely the person I know that supposedly cares about the shit I do. Instead I'm sitting alone eating goddamn pickles.

Let's just run through the list of recent events: a capital x slashed into my chest, regular visits to cult group meetings, which may serve exceptional baked goods but also weird me out, spending quality time with Seth Cromwell, the man everybody fears like he's the damn Night Stalker, and oh yeah, running around naked in the white world after a weird isolation tank session.

Shouldn't I have someone to talk to about this for Christ's sake? Why am I doing this alone? It doesn't make sense anymore. There is no point.

I hold still a moment, and I can hear the clock on the kitchen wall ticking.

I'm all alone.

Doesn't anyone actually want to be with me? Did she ever really care? Why did I start believing in all of this kind of crap again?

I take a deep breath.

The peanut butter is long gone, so I get the pickles back out to cap the meal with a final spear. It doesn't cleanse my pallet so much as scorch the hell out of that shit.

One thing Glenn does have is a shit ton of coffee. I dump some extra dark beans in the grinder and jam the button down a few times. The bag boasts of this blend's cocoa nib after taste, which I'm anxious to try. It kind of smells like tobacco, though.

I catch my reflection in the window as I move to the coffee machine. And that first blink is one of those weird moments where my own face surprises me. I see myself when I'm not at all expecting it, and I don't just see what I expect to see. I see myself as foreign for that first fraction of a second. I see myself the way a stranger must see me. An imperfection in the glass warps my face so one cheek bone looks bigger than the other.

And the fact that I am here alone gorging myself with pickles and coffee becomes more real.

And I'm not even mad anymore. I'm not.

Just please, please come here now. Call me. Anything. Don't leave me here alone.

I put the pickles away, and I sit in the quiet. The clock ticks. Please.

I close my eyes. I try to will my mind to go blank, but I can't do it. It just keeps circling back to this despair, this neediness that I don't even recognize in myself. This desire to plead, to beg, that I want to erase and can't.

I stand up and go to the living room like I can walk away from the feeling somehow. Now the kitchen clock is the tiniest pulse in the distance. My thoughts still spiral through the same progression in this new room, of course. I can't shut it off.

I turn off the light and sit in the dark, shoulders leaned back into the couch cushions and chin angled up toward the ceiling. There are no stars above, though. There is only the dark. I guess this is where I always end up.

Awake in the dark. Alone.

Please.

Please.

Please.

I feel like I should be able to float away from this. I should be able to drift off to some other plane because this one is too painful for me to exist in. Because no one should have to feel this way. I know other people must, but I think they can just forget it or something. It always sticks with me, though. It marks me up good.

Or maybe they don't let themselves feel it all the way. Their subconscious does some sleight of hand to keep them safe from themselves. I don't have that ability somehow. I feel all of it.

And the purr of a car engine outside interrupts the silence. I sit upright to listen. A car door slams. After a pause, the key slips into the lock on the front door with the clink and grind of metal on metal, and the deadbolt retracts with a snap.

I watch the door swing into the room, and Louise steps into the opening. She hovers there in the threshold a moment, kicking off her shoes before she closes the door.

She strides into the dark of the living room, her head angled toward the floor. Even after she flips on the lamp, she seems so lost in thought that she doesn't realize I'm sitting there for a full second.

"Oh, hey. I didn't think you were home," she says. "Why are you sitting out here in the dark?"

"Yeah, hey," I say. "I don't know."

"Well, you could have said 'hi,'" she says. "I mean, you must have watched me walk in."

"Yeah, sorry," I say. "I was thinking, I guess."

She walks out toward the kitchen as she goes on.

"Well, Woods knows nothing," she says. "He got all excited once I got around to mentioning Farber's disappearing corpse act."

"Same with Cromwell," I say.

I hear the fridge open and shut about two seconds later.

"Yikes," she says. "We need to go to the grocery store at some point."

"I know," I say.

The ascending melody of running water filling a glass echoes off of the walls. She walks back into the living room and sits next to me.

"Are you all right?" she says.

"Yeah," I say.

She stares at me.

"You just seem quiet is all," she says.

"Sorry," I say.

She hugs herself against my shoulder.

"I missed you," she says.

But it's not real. It's not real. I can't take it. I want to pull away. I want to float away. Instead I say:

"Me too."

"It's not so late," she says, her head leaning on me. "We could still go do something fun tonight, if you feel like it."

I don't feel like it. I feel like disappearing. All of these words are wind. All of these feelings are lies. I'd be better off erased, really, my existence wiped away like I was never even here at all.

"I guess a bunch of people are going to Up and Under tonight," she says.

Here we go. An invitation to a sports bar that a bunch of college kids hang out at. Maybe it will be like an episode of Cheers. Taking a break from all of my troubles sure would help a lot, right? We can drink Jägerbombs with frat guys and shit. Play some darts.

It's too much. It's too much. Take me out of this place. I want to go away.

I clench my teeth and my fists and my brain, and the familiar tidal wave arrives with a crash as the white world opens in my head.

- 23 -

I lead the way into the lawn care section, Louise pushing the cart behind me. The floor is made of egg again, a three to four inch layer of hardboiled egg white flooring, I'd say. I bounce on the balls of my feet for a second just to feel the squish.

"You looking into a weed whacker purchase?" she says.

"Hell yeah," I say.

I rip one down from its display and brandish it with my maggot hands, mock whacking the bags of grass seed below, complete with awesome sound effects. I get a little carried away, though, and knock over several bottles of some kind of fertilizer.

"Calm down," Louise says. She takes the weed whacker from me and puts it back.

"Calmer than you are," I say.

"What's gotten into you?" she says.

"The holy spirit," I say.

She just stares at me.

"What? I'm just in a good mood," I say.

We move past a bunch of lawn mowers and rakes. There's even a little display of snow shovels for the impending winter.

Something about the lighting in here is so weird, manipulated. I remember reading that they light these stores a really particular way to make it as comfortable as possible to encourage sales. They lower the lighting in the lingerie section, for example, to help people relax around a bunch of panties and all. Fruits and vegetables look better in natural light. Meat looks tired in natural light, though, and fares better under bright white light. And so on. Every store and department has their own illumination strategy for separating you from as much of your money as they can.

"Didn't we come here to get groceries?" Louise says, interrupting my thoughts.

"We're browsing," I say.

"Come on. Are you actually considering buying those tiki torches?" she says.

It's not until she says this that I realize I'm holding two tiki torches, one in each hand. I don't say anything. I just put the torches back all smooth and do the nonchalant shrug.

We walk past the electronics, but it's not that interesting to me. I want to pick stuff up, concrete items I can touch and consider. Everything cool in the electronics section is locked behind glass or wrapped in plastic.

As we move into the hardware section, my limbs seem to get heavier and heavier, like they're filling with sand with every step I take. I lift my arm to test it, and it shakes a little, so I drop it back down before Louise can see this. I lean up against a shelf in the aisle where all of the wrenches and hammers hang.

"Now what?" Louise says.

"Hang on," I say. "I feel sick."

After I say it, I realize that I do feel pretty sick. My hand clutches my gut. I lean forward a little, expecting gallons of fluid to come cascading out of my mouth like a waterfall.

Instead, nothing happens.

"Let's go," Louise says. "The groceries are this way."

She leads us past a bunch of pillows and a shelf of beach towels with Justin Bieber's face on them. My legs don't feel heavy at all now, at least. I lift my arms, and they're all light now. Weird how these things seem to come and go.

We stop momentarily when I grab a Panini press and shove it in the cart. Louise puts it back. We're in an aisle of junk appliances such as – an electric ice shaver, a quesadilla maker, an electric can opener, and my favorite, the breakfast sandwich maker. The two outer chambers toast the English muffin and melt the cheese. The middle chamber fries an egg. Then you remove the plate under the egg, and bam, your sandwich is made.

"I already have a breakfast sandwich maker," I say. "It's called a frying pan."

We enter the grocery area near the cookie aisle. The lighting here is different than the hardware and Panini press aisle. More natural, I think.

On sight, I throw some Oreos in the cart, Double Stufs, the way Glenn would've wanted it. If it were possible to pour a little out of a 40 ounce of liquid Oreo right here in the store in honor of my missing friend, I would do that.

The next thing I know, we're stalking down the foreign foods aisle, and let's just say I'm handling a lot of the merchandise. I discover about 17 Asian sauces I want to try, some weird Mexican drink mix that's made of chocolate and cinnamon, two flavors of ramen noodles I was previously unfamiliar with and a jar of Mario Batali vodka sauce that runs about six times what the other jars of marinara cost. All of this gets twisted about in my hands and then tossed in the cart. When I turn around, though, Louise has put most of it back.

"Stop messing around," she says. "You need to get stuff for meals, not just sauces."

She seems to be finding it all at least somewhat humorous, though. She thinks I'm joking. What she doesn't realize is that I never joke around about Asian cuisine.

Ever.

Seriously, though, it seems a bit insane that she has no sense of my state, but maybe it's for the best. Maybe.

And for a second, reality bleeds through, and I see the real color of things. I feel lost, adrift, surrounded by people that I can't connect with and can't connect with me.

Then I spot the ice cream and practically sprint to the freezer door with all of the Ben and Jerry's behind it. My maggoty hands press on the glass, and my nose hovers a few inches shy of touching it as well.

I decide to limit myself to three flavors for the sake of propriety. Cherry Garcia goes without saying as flavor number one. Right now I'm thinking Chubby Hubby for number two, but I'm wavering a little on that one. I like the peanut butter swirl a lot, but the chocolate covered pretzel bits are a little on the massive side and not that tasty. For number three, I'll have to take a dive into the ice cream abyss and get something I've never tried before.

I realize Louise has been talking for a while, and I totally missed it, lost in ice cream land.

"I think I'm going with Milk and Cookies," she says.

Genius. She is a genius.

She reaches into the freezer and pulls free the pint,

smudging finger marks into the frost running around the side of the carton. Now it's my turn to brave the cold. I open the freezer door and lean in.

"Maybe you should just pick one," she says, just as I get the third pint tucked inside my elbow. "We can always get more next time."

True. True.

I put back the Chubby Hubby and, to my surprise, the Cherry Garcia. I'm going off the beaten path this eve. I'm going with Karamel Sutra. Half caramel ice cream, half chocolate ice cream with chocolate chunks and a core of molten caramel. Ok, it's not molten, but still…

We walk the aisles a while longer. I kind of wish this would never end.

I lie in bed, awake in the dark like always. The white is fading a bit, but I still feel pleasant enough. Louise sleeps next to me.

I try to replay the evening in my mind, but I can't quite get my head back to that place I was right before I went to the white world. I can only replay the shininess of Wal-Mart.

I know I hurt before that, but I can't remember exactly what it was like. I can't remember the feel of it.

I suppose it doesn't matter much. I can always get away, right? I can always make it OK, so what is there to worry about?

- 24 -

The next morning I'm awakened by my phone beeping – a text from Babinaux. Apparently she's stopping by in about 20 minutes, and it's important. I want to lie back and let the blankets hug me longer, and I consider doing so. Instead, I rise from the bed anyway and stumble toward the shower. I don't recall choosing this action, but I lean my head forward and go with the momentum.

En route, I kick a crushed Ben and Jerry's carton. Wow, so somebody was partying pretty hard last night. I guess I really got after that Karamel Sutra. It's just a foggy memory now. Maybe it means I've finally built up a tolerance for eating and drinking while in the white world.

I turn on the water, adjusting the temp. I guess I'm pretty used to this beastly water pressure by now. Just don't let it make direct contact with the genitals, and you're fine. I should make a sign that says that to hang in here.

As I towel off, I get a single flash of that feeling I had just before the world went white last evening, a pang of vulnerability and panic and nausea climbing my throat.

But now I'm numb again, the colors of the world muted ever so faintly.

I dress, and by the time I get out to the living room, Babinaux is already there, sitting on the couch. Guess I left the door unlocked, too. Between that and pounding down the ice cream, I'm really turning into a bad boy type like Charlie Sheen or something.

Babinaux looks up from her phone as I enter the room. She smiles and points to the paper cup of coffee on the table as she says:

"Good morning."

"Morning," I say, scooping up the beverage. "And thank you."

I take a sip. Another crazy concoction, though I think it's caramel instead of cinnamon this time. Now this might be because I ate about 1600 calories of caramel ice cream last night, but I think the cinnamon was better.

"Are you feeling ok?" she says.

"Yeah," I say. "I'm great."

She frowns.

"You don't look so great," she says.

She squints and leans forward to get a better look.

"Thanks," I say. "What do you mean?"

"Your eyes look all puffed up," she says.

I press my index and middle finger to each of my eyes. My right eyelid is actually a little tender, swollen and painful to the touch. I guess I was too tired to get much of a look in the mirror.

"Must be some kind allergy thing," I say.

"Well, if you're feeling up to it," she says, leaning back. "Randy wants you to do the third initiation tonight."

"And what will that entail?" I say.

"First there is a feast," she says.

"I can get behind that," I say. "What else?"

She hesitates.

"I probably shouldn't tell you the exact details," she says. "But there's a ritual reenacting your spiritual rebirth."

"Like a baptism?" I say.

"Sort of," she says.

I try to read into her expression, but she is stoic as always.

"Well, many of us will be there for the meal, myself included, and he said there will be four of you doing the actual ritual this time," she says. "It's not as rare as the water ritual."

"Well, whatever," I say. "I guess I may as well do it."

She had me at "feast."

"How are things with you and Louise?" she says.

"Good, I think," I say. "Maybe. I don't know."

"What's wrong?" she says.

I plan to say little, but the words pour out of me like water rushing out of the mouth of a downspout during a storm.

"It's my fault. I feel like I can never shut my brain off and just be," I say. "So say, for example, she doesn't get back to me right away when I call, I start freaking out. At first I'm all mad, but then after a while I'm just pining for her affection. Feeling lonely and abandoned and stranded. It's really pathetic. By the time she actually comes around, I've twisted myself around so much that I'm actually resentful toward her for finally showing."

I tap at my pant leg.

"I guess it feels like she put me through all of that, even though I know that's not the truth," I say. "And then another part of me just doesn't believe her anymore. Like I pine after her affection and then reject it when it comes. I see it as not real, all phony like she's pretending or maybe fooling herself.

Does that make sense?"

She tilts her head.

"Well, it makes sense in that I understand what you mean," she says. "It doesn't make much sense, though, as far as a way for a person to behave. I mean, it's pretty irrational, no?"

"Well, yeah," I say. "I get what you mean."

"Have you tried talking to her about it?" she says.

"No," I say. "I guess I should do that."

"I would say so," Babinaux says.

"Sometimes it's hard to talk," I say.

"I understand," she says. "But a lack of communication is like cancer for a relationship. It grows and grows until it kills its host. If you don't talk to her about all of the stuff bouncing around in your head, it will only grow. It will only isolate you from her more and more."

We're quiet for a moment.

"He could never accept love," she says. "My friend I told you about, I mean. He never learned how to accept love. I don't want that to happen to you."

- 25 -

I get to the church early, and judging from the lack of cars in the lot, no one else is here yet. I stroll around the grounds for a bit, circling the dead trees tinted green with lichen. With a little more daylight than the last time I was out here, I notice that the grass is coming up on ankle deep. I wonder who mows this. Does the League pay somebody to come out here and mow around a building they barely use?

I meander toward the door as I contemplate these maintenance matters. It's unlocked, which doesn't shock me. I wasn't planning on going in until someone else arrived, but I guess I will.

It's an eerie feeling to walk around in an empty church. Padding across the blood red carpet so many have walked on before, I get a sense of the building's history. There's an energy here, a past that vibrates in the air, that you can feel in your chest. This room meant a lot to people for decades before I was even born. It was sacred to them. It was a pillar that held up their community. And now it's being used for some pretty weird shit as it crumbles. But that's better than not being used at all, I think. I guess I can't speak to how they might feel about it.

I work my way past the pews and poke around the sanctuary. Under a bench, I spot a box of ancient microphones.

Ribbon and dynamic mics with the grills beat to hell. I bet some are valuable, even with the scuffs and dents. People love vintage audio equipment.

There's a stack of old hymnals in the corner. I pick one up to find that it's falling apart, the spine of the book disintegrating, so big chunks of pages pull away from each other. Gold lettering on the cover says it was published in 1898. I flip through the pages the best I can and read the song titles. I feel like the word "majesty" was a lot more popular back then.

"You in the mood to sing for us?" a voice says from the back of the room.

I look up. It's Randy.

"Not really," I say. "Unless you're offering to tickle those ivories over there."

I point at the piano and wiggle my fingers on the imaginary keyboard in front of me. Randy does not seem amused, so I guess it wasn't that funny. I bet if you're old you've heard "tickle the ivories" throughout your life, so it's not an obscure reference or anything like that. I really need to better tailor my material to the elderly for events like this.

"At least you're on time," he says.

What the hell? I swear it wasn't long ago that Randy clearly thought I was awesome. He praised my passion and so forth. Well, I guess that honeymoon is over, because now he's belittling me left and right.

"I heard there will be a feast," I say.

"You heard right," he says.

He walks out of the room and heads downstairs, ending our conversation without telling me a single culinary detail. I'm pretty sure that in some parts of the world, confirming a feast without elaborating on the menu is considered treason. I will let it slide – I'm a merciful Grobnagger - but still…

I think about going downstairs to check out whatever might already be set up food-wise, but I decide I'd rather not be around Randy. That level of grumpiness is infectious. I'm trying to keep a positive frame of mind, get my food, and get out of here.

I sit on one of the folding chairs in the sanctuary. There are two rows of seven of them, which I'm guessing were used for a choir at some point. Facing the pews, I watch the front door. People trickle through, many of them toting casserole dishes and crock pots heavy with food. The mix of smells is interesting – I detect at least a couple varieties of baked beans and some form of fried chicken, but some of the other spices and combinations are hard to place, which makes them all the more enticing. My mouth lubes itself up pretty good during all of this smelling.

I recognize a few of the people entering from the blood ceremony, and I spot Janice from the meetings at Randy's, but others I've never seen before. It's an older crowd on the whole, and a smiley crowd on top of that. These ladies carting in the food, in particular, beam at me like I'm Ryan Seacrest or some other guy that older ladies like a lot. My point is that I'm pretty sure me and Seacrest could have our way with many of these women, but we are both gentlemen.

After a while, the stream of people entering slows to a stop, and I hear a growing rumble roll up from the basement - the tangled mess of conversations piled on top of each other. I ease myself off of the chair and get a good stretch in. I like to get limbered up before a feast like this. The last thing you want to do is pull something before you're able to complete the meal.

I move down the stairs, and I feel like a kid walking into an adult party by himself. There are a few rows of tables in the middle of the room for sitting, and then a line of tables running around half of the perimeter of the room sporting quite an impressive spread of homemade dishes and desserts.

It looks like people are starting to get around to fix plates of food for themselves as I step foot on the basement floor. They are forming a line along the food tables, so no one seems to notice me. This is good. Lids get pulled off of dishes in rapid succession like this is the reveal stage at the end of all of the magic tricks at once. Little clouds of steam puff everywhere, and the multitude of vapors intertwine in the air to create an intense smell that I want to call mystical.

I slip into the line unnoticed and try to keep my head down. I grab a plate once I'm close enough, and it's straight out of a school cafeteria – plastic with five rectangular segments, a big one for the entrée and four smaller ones for sides. I do like that it has more total real estate than your average pot luck plate, which might be disposable plastic or paper. Whoever is calling these kinds of shots for the League, that person gets it. This is how you build something special with your cult.

That said, I still only have five segments for my first run through. I'll need to be selective.

My first choice is a pasta salad with chunks of feta in it. I figure anybody taking the time to crumble some feta in there is not fucking around. Next up, I get some biscuits that look insane, fluffy as hell. An old lady with a wig the shade of cherry shoe polish nods at me as I take one, so I take two and she closes her eyes and nods even more emphatically.

For the protein, I opt to keep it simple with some fried chicken. I guess I have to get a vegetable now, so I go for some green beans that seem popular. And last but not least? Mashed potatoes with gravy. Duh.

I turn toward the seating area, and I see a few people gawking, but they look more intrigued than anything. Then I spot Babinaux waving at me from her seat in the corner, so I head that way.

She eyes my plate as I approach.

"Lotta starch, Jeffrey," she says.

"What?" I say. "Oh."

I look down at my plate. Looks tasty enough to me, starch or no.

"You know, they have this new thing called salad," she says. "Rumored to be good for you."

She takes a bite of something green and leafy.

"Oh, this is only the beginning," I say. "This is phase one. Maybe I'll feel like something light like a salad when I go back for thirds or fourths."

I tear into the food like a dog tearing into some food. I don't know. I'm not always that great with similes. In any case, I eat in a way that not only makes me feel guilty but likely brings shame to the rest of my family as well. If you can curse your family through sheer expression of gluttony, I fear I have done so today. So that's something I'll have to live with.

After my dessert plate – peach pie, blueberry pie bars, chocolate cheesecake and homemade oatmeal cream pies – I go in for a coffee. Now I'm not actually in the mood for coffee, and as you can imagine, I'm quite full. I've come up with a plan, though. I feel like dumping a mug or two of black coffee onto that pile of calories in my gut might kick start the process of breaking the food down and give me the upper hand in the impending intestinal battle ahead of me.

It's risky, but it just might work.

I sit down with great care to avoid bursting at the seams – not the seams of my clothes, the seams of my body. Once I'm down, I plan to stay that way for a good hour as motion of any kind would only incite discord in my digestive tract.

Some of the older people go about cleaning up, and looking over the others, I start to get a sense of who will be going through this "symbolic spiritual rebirth" with me. There are a couple of girls near my age that appear to be sisters that I suspect will be rebirthing pretty hard in a bit here. They look like they're not of this era. I don't mean that as a slight or anything – they're not ugly. They just look like young versions of someone's grandma somehow or maybe more like a picture in an old photo album. It's not the way they dress, though, it's how they handle themselves and their facial features.

On the other side of the room, there's a guy with thick stubble that sticks out as well. His face wears a blank expression and does not waver from it. I'd say he's probably 30 to 35.

Randy starts working his way around the room, flitting from table to table to tap someone on the shoulder here or whisper something in someone else's ear there. Those tapped rise and move with purpose. He moves to the stubble guy and talks to him, so that pretty much confirms my suspicion. We're about to do this, I believe.

This isn't perfect. I hoped we'd have another half an hour of a post meal breather. I know my belly will put up a fight.

Randy moves toward me, and I try to send mind bullets at

him – not to kill him or even injure him seriously – just to graze a leg and slow him down or something. The mind bullets go wide of the target, however. I've yet to actually hit anything with them.

He leans over when he reaches me, and his breath smells exactly like Boston baked beans with extra onions on top.

"It's time," he says. "Meet me and the others by my car."

I stand the way I imagine an early model android will stand – very stiff in the waist and hips. Stuff gurgles in my gut right away, something large shifts deep in the bowels, and the shame and guilt well inside of me again.

I eyeball the stainless steel coffee dispenser and contemplate dumping another cup of black down in there to try to take a proactive approach, but another part of me sees it more like pouring gas on a fire, so I do nothing. Sometimes there's no quick fix. You've got to take responsibility for what you've done and accept the consequences.

I walk with a gait that I believe minimizes the chances of anal leakage, though I don't have a lot of experience in this area. Squirting may not be a strong possibility at this juncture, but those that don't prepare themselves always get hit the hardest. It's like I always say: Hope for the best, prepare for the anal leakage.

Passing through the basement seems easy enough. My shuffling trot keeps me feeling secure and seems to go unnoticed from what I can tell. As I near the edge of the room, though, it occurs to me that the stairs are going to be a problem – possibly a big brown one.

I try to take the first step sort of sideways as I feel like that will involve less hip and thigh movement. It's harder to step sideways with much of your body clenched up tighter than a clam shell, however. My foot clubs around the step without ever getting high enough to mount it.

Then it dawns on me that because of all of the old people often at church, there are two hand rails here-one on each side. I can lift myself up a step at a time with my arms. It's genius.

I lift and step and lift and step until I make it to the top. My instinct is to laugh at top volume while I do this. I feel like if I draw a lot of attention to my odd behavior people are more likely to interpret it as goofing around. I get some weird looks, but it could have been worse.

I trudge through the nave and out the door toward Randy's car, my middle churning liquid like my intestines have been tasked with fermenting some kind of prison hooch. I see the girls from a different era in the parking lot, but they're standing by someone else's car. Not sure what to make of that.

Stubble walks up to Randy's car as silent as a ninja, so I don't see him approaching. He just appears there next to me. And then I figure it out. We're riding separately. Me and Stubs will ride with Randy, while the ladies are taking a ladymobile.

I say hi to him, and he grunts. Somehow I don't think Stubs is much of a conversationalist.

Before I even know Randy is in the vicinity, Stubs calls shotgun, and I wheel around to see the old man just stepping though the doorway. So I guess this guy gets real chatty when it counts.

Randy hugs his arms around a big cardboard box, but I can't tell what's in it. Looks heavy. He rotates his wrist to point his keys at the car and pop the trunk. He strides toward it, presumably to load the box in.

"Get in," he says.

Upon settling in the backseat, the tectonic plates in my lower abdomen shift, and the churning slows down. I think I've navigated past the danger zone, and it should be smooth gut sailing from here on in. This comes with a feeling of accomplishment. The sea was awfully angry today.

Randy says little when he gets into the car. He just starts it up and drives.

With no talk and no radio, it's pretty quiet in here, the kind of quiet that harbors a nervous energy. It's a Prius, so there's barely even any engine noise. I want to ask a few questions, but the atmosphere in the vehicle is stifling, so I hold off. Air sucking through the sliver of an opening in Randy's window creates the soundtrack, which is fitting since this pretty much sucks.

We ride out past woods and field after field of corn and soy beans and brush. It's interesting how far you can see looking over a field, especially as you rise up on a small hill. The plants stretch on and on until somewhere out there the dusk swallows them up.

The car slows as we take a left onto a dirt road, and I realize it's been quite a while since I've seen a building of any type. There was a rotting barn back there somewhere, but that was a while ago. Now that I think about it, I don't see the ladymobile behind us. I guess maybe Randy is a bit of speed demon.

But then I remember that scene in Casino where Joe Pesci gets driven out into some rural cornfield area, and his voice over internal monologue is interrupted midsentence by the sound of one of the guys cracking him with an aluminum baseball bat. He never sees it coming.

Though I don't know Stubs all that well, I can't see Randy beating me to death with a baseball bat. It's like I always say, though: Hope for the best, prepare to be pummeled to death.

Yeah, I probably shouldn't recycle my material so frequently.

Anyway, Randy takes it real slow on the dirt road. Rocks kick up in all directions and clang out steel drum noises when they hit the undercarriage. Not much of a melody, but with the radio off, it's almost good enough to pass for music.

We inch down the slit of dirt bisecting a field of overgrown weeds gone to seed. The beige blades of grass sway in the breeze in clusters that collectively form odd shapes and patterns. It looks like people at a stadium doing the wave but more chaotic.

And then we're climbing a small hill, the lack of speed adding a sense of suspense. I think I know what will be at the top, though: more grass. We ascend and ascend for quite some time, mimicking a sloth climbing a tree.

At the top, I see that I was right: more grass, indeed. Sorry to spoil that for you.

No, wait. There's something poking out from the top of the plant life. Something gray and roundish, but I can't see much of it. It almost looks like a trash can with a wooden frame above it from here.

We draw closer, and there's just enough sunlight left to discern that it's stone. Then it clicks – a well.

I'd think that we'd blow right past such an ordinary field item at the speed of a tortoise, but I can see now the road leads right to it and ends.

Interesting. I thought I already did the water ritual.

The Prius saunters up near the well and parks. Again, Randy doesn't say anything, he just gets out and pops the trunk. Stubs doesn't move, but I decide to get out and stretch my legs.

As I rise, there's one last gurgle of prison hooch sloshing about inside of me like a rogue wave, and then things settle once more. I take a few paces out of the car, my feet grinding pebbles into the dirt road. I raise my arms out to the sides and rotate my neck back and forth to try to loosen everything from the shoulder blades up a little.

Then I turn to get a look at what Randy has in the trunk. It's on the edge of getting dark out, so at first I only see the red of a couple of gas cans. Then Randy pulls a shadowy garment out of the box. I glean that it's a robe as he slips it on over his clothes.

I'm guessing we'll get dressed up in our robes, draw a little water out of the old well, splash it on our foreheads, say some sacred words and be done with it. So I mosey over to the well to take a gander. The first thing that strikes me? It's huge. I'm no well expert, but this one is a good 8 or 10 feet across. Seems big to me. I find a large wooden crate instead of a bucket. It dangles just below the lip of the wall up against the side closest to me. The rope suspending it runs up to a pulley attached to the wooden frame over the well. It looks very sturdy, the crate, and there are gaps between the boards, so it would suck ass at hauling up any water.

Well, that doesn't make sense. Randy must have another trick up that robe sleeve of his.

The second thing that catches my attention is the odor. I get a whiff of something chemical. I want to say it smells like witch hazel, but I barely even remember what that smells like.

Going back over to the car, I hear the two of them mumbling. They both sport their robes. I go to grab mine from the box, but before I get there, Randy closes the trunk.

"You forgetting something?" I say.

"Get undressed," he says.

"What? Don't I need a robe?" I say.

Randy doesn't look straight at me.

"You need to be undressed," he says. "It's part of the ritual."

"What about this guy?" I say, pointing at Stubs.

"You're going first," he says. "He'll go second."

I try to find a good angle to argue this. I could refuse, but with all of this new stuff about the missing body, I probably need my League contacts more than ever. I could run, just live out here off of corn and soybeans until the pesticide kills me.

"Alright," I say.

I go behind the well and strip down. Really, Randy has seen me naked almost as much as my girlfriend at this point, which I did not foresee back when we first met. Back then, he was just a guy that looked like Dumbledore. It was a simpler time.

When I turn around, Randy and Stubs approach with lanterns aflame at their sides. Their hoods are up so I can't see their faces. I cup my dick and balls in my hand and sort of waddle in their direction, stopping a few feet short because, you know, I'm naked.

Randy waves me over the rest of the way, though I can only tell it's him by the white hair on his knuckles. He directs me to stand between the two of them, and the three of us face the well. They set the lanterns down in unison.

When Randy speaks, his voice takes on a quality I haven't

heard from him before – a vocal projection so loud and thick, it's almost hoarse sounding. I hate to mix wizards here, but it kind of sounds like when Gandalf yells at the Balrog.

"We are born into this world naked, innocent," he says. "And so shall ye be reborn."

I would probably say "Check," here as a joke, but the Gandalf voice is too intense to mess with. I don't want him to yell at me like I'm a fool of a Took.

"We are born into this world blind, unaware," he says. "And so shall ye be reborn."

He pulls out a strip of fabric, but it's not until he's fastening it to my head that I realize it's a blindfold.

So that's good.

"We are born into this world from the dark to the light," he says. "And so shall ye be reborn."

We're cutting it a little close on this one, considering it's getting dark now. Of course, behind the blindfold, I can no longer confirm this with my eyes.

A hand on each side of me takes my hand. Randy's is cold and dry, Stubs' is all clammy. They pull me along a few paces, and now we're at the well.

"We've got you," Randy says. "On 3, take a step up."

There's a pause. I probably should have gone with that running plan a while ago.

"One."

I suddenly have to piss.

"Two."

Really bad.

"Three."

I step up onto the edge of the well, totter for a second, but they help me get my balance.

"Now step down into the well," Randy says. "On 3."

"What?" I say.

"You're stepping into the crate," he says. "You'll step with one foot until you feel the crate under you, then step with the other. We'll have you the whole time."

"Maybe I should take the blindfold off first," I say. "Might help."

Nobody speaks, but I think I hear Stubs snicker.

"It's a leap to faith," Randy says.

I don't know whether to correct him for saying "to" rather than "of" or "leap" when I'm stepping. I mean, I'm stepping or plunging, there will be no leaps, I can tell you that.

"One."

Oh yeah, pee feeling again. Almost forgot.

"Two."

My bladder is about to burst.

"Three."

I step down, feel the wood plank under my foot.

"You've got it," Randy says. "Now grab the rope and step with the other foot."

He lets go. And I'm tipping forward. I reach out for the rope, but it finds me instead, my chest and torso ramming into it, flinging the crate crashing into the wall. My other hand wrenches free of Stubs' grip as I fall. And the crate doesn't feel solid under me. I know I'm about to fall the rest of the way when my hands find the rope and grip it. Everything totters a bit and then stabilizes under me. I'm squatting in the crate, choking the rope the best I can.

"What the fuck?" I say.

"You're fine," Randy says.

I rip the blindfold off just as the crate begins its descent. The pulley groans as the rope scrapes over it, and the circle of dusk gets smaller and smaller above. And I realize that chemical smell is stronger now. Much stronger. It's not witch hazel, I think now. It's familiar, but something is off about it. Maybe it's just so unexpected here that I can't place it.

The crate touches down on the bottom. So it's a dry well after all. The smell is overpowering. Could it be-

Voices above interrupt my thoughts. They sound so tiny now. Are they talking to me?

"What?" I say.

"Get out of the crate," Randy says. His voice echoes in a way that makes the volume swell later in the delivery, making the last word the loudest. It's strange.

Wait. Did he say get out of the crate?

"What?" I say.

"It's a simple display of faith, Jeffrey," he says. "Now step out."

After the letting go incident, I have little trust in Randy. I hesitate.

"Look, you step off," he says. "We yank it back up here and in a half an hour we pull you out. It's that simple."

I hate to do it, but I step out of the crate. As I watch it ascend to the tiny circle of half light up there, I think over and over again that this was a huge mistake. At last, it's gone. No more squeaking pulley. No more crate up there. Nothing.

The chemical smell is pretty unbelievable, and I feel light headed. I sit down in the dark and concentrate to keep my eyes from drifting closed. I can hear my heartbeat in my ears.

And then a few drops hit me, wetness. I figure rain, but it stings, and it stinks. And then it's more than droplets, it's gushing down.

I yell. It's wordless and powerless and small. Scrambling back to get away, I bump into a bucket and knock it over. Liquid gushes everywhere, and I feel around, and there are more of buckets all around the perimeter of the well. And I know now that the stuff raining down, and the stuff down here making that smell are one and the same.

It's not water. It's gasoline, possibly mixed with some other flammable fluid so I couldn't quite place the smell.

And then the pouring stops, and I look up. I can't quite see straight, I guess from the fumes.

But I spot a light fluttering down toward me, all slowed down. It looks like a firefly coasting down to check things out. But as it gets closer, the image comes clear – a wooden match tumbling end over end.

In the split second before it hits, I picture the burned body in the vacant lot. I see the eye socket where the melted skin re-congealed. I see the permanent smile framed by blackened lips. I see the shriveled man reduced from flesh to ash.

And the match hits, and the fire flashes so bright it almost looks white, and it's everywhere, and it's on me, crawling hot up onto my chest, my face, heat searing all of me. Every nerve ending wails as loud as it can, all shrill.

I feel my skin drying and cracking on my arms first, flesh gone black. My entire body flails, and the back of my head cracks into something solid - the wall, I guess. I flop onto the ground, and I try to roll a little, but it's no use. Everything is covered in a blaze of gas. I can see only fire in all directions, flames billowing up and up, and that shimmer of heat distortion like I'm watching it all through imperfect glass.

It sounds like wind roaring with periodic crackles and pops of things being broken down by heat, of me being broken down and sizzling.

And I smell it. I smell my hair first, like something rotten consumed by flames, and then the stench of my charred and melting flesh hits my nostrils. It smells like pork chops blackening on a too hot grill, the outside charring immediately with the inside left raw. The image pops into my head for a split second - juicy fat dripping out of a rack of ribs, tumbling between the bars to the flames below.

And I go to scream, but when I open my mouth and inhale the flaming vapor sucks between my lips and enters my throat and lungs in a flash. And the fire steals my breath, and the scorch fills my chest. And I choke, and I feel my throat collapse into wet flaps of melt, and I want to cough, but I can't. I can't. It's caught. It's stuck in what used to be my throat and what used to be my lungs.

And then everything fades to white.

- 26 -

The white shines everywhere. It is everything, and it is perfect, and I am nothing.

But I am here. I am thinking. I am conscious. I can't be nothing.

I am small, though. I am one tiny piece of everything, then, one ray of light shining with all of the rest.

I don't know. Maybe something like that.

Maybe what I used to be is nothing. That might make more sense.

I was something but now I am everything, one piece of it, anyway.

And it's not so bad when you look at it that way.

- 27 -

I wake in a grass field, the world gone white around me. I wriggle my maggot fingers in front of me and laugh. How to even describe it, I feel so complete, and I feel no pain. I throb with pleasure. It hugs me. It holds me. Everything makes sense. The universe makes sense, and I am everywhere and nowhere, and it is perfect.

I rise from the ground, and it strikes me that I'm not naked anymore. My normal clothes adorn my body – t-shirt, jeans, hoodie, hat, sunglasses.

I like it. I like to feel covered up. My feet are bare, though, which seems a little weird.

Looking around, it's just grass as far as I can see with one huge tree standing way in the distance. The grass stands about knee high, but it's not all scraggly and whatever. It's even and symmetrical and seems to shift in the air in unison, like the whole field is inhaling and exhaling. And I realize that it's green. Even though the world has been bled white, this grass shines bright green. It seems so natural somehow that I didn't even consider it at first.

And so I stride through it, thousands of blades reaching out to brush the legs of my pants. It swishes around me, and it chills the skin on my feet where it makes contact, brisk but refreshing. I'm thankful to be barefoot to feel this, to experience the frosty touch of these plants.

I walk toward the tree. There's nothing else to go for, I guess. It's far, though. The clear air and flat land mean I can see a long way, of course, but the tree branches reach up into the heavens. I can't see the top. It's difficult to express the scale of this. The trunk girth seems impossible, but I'll withhold judgment until I get a little closer. Interestingly, from here, at least, I only see wood. I don't see any leaves.

The air moves here. It's not like wind, exactly, or at least it's not like any wind I've ever felt before. It pulses too evenly, and it doesn't build and recede like wind. It's just on full blast and then off with no in between.

The air gusts in, cool and heavy. It has some wet to it, but it's not sticky like a humid day in the summer. It's a little too cool for that, I guess. It feels more like walking into a basement, the way the air takes on some substance, some texture.

I jog for a bit to try to gain on the tree, but it's hard to tell if I'm getting any closer, so I go back to walking. Probably best to save my energy, even if jogging didn't seem to tire me so much.

Just like that, I come upon a dirt trail, well worn, running perpendicular to my path to the tree. Never saw it coming until I stepped onto it. I stop and stand on it a moment. The sand is warm underfoot, as though the sun shines down upon it, but when I look up I find no sun in the sky, just white everywhere.

Looking both ways, I see nothing but trail and grass stretching on and on. I have no real desire to follow it. The tree seems much more intriguing.

I move on, entering the field on the opposite side of the trail. The grass feels different here, almost like it's trying to stick to my feet. Not in a slimy or gooey way so much as the way a grasshopper's leg kind of attaches itself to your skin. It's almost like Velcro somehow. It presses itself onto me and latches on with its little ridges, and with each step I just pry away from it and move forward. It's not the worst feeling, but it is not pleasant. I feel a sense of it being gluttonous, and that sort of grosses me out.

And for some reason it pops into my head that people in caskets are barefoot. They put that blanket over their feet, so you never really think about it, but they don't wear shoes and socks when they're buried.

I stop. The tiniest pin prick of fear penetrates my brain, entering just above the brain stem. I try to remember where I was just before this. I close my eyes, and I let my mind reach out for it. It delves into whatever ether memories are stored in. But all it comes back with is the image of fried chicken and biscuits and green beans and mashed potatoes smothered in gravy. Pretty sure I ate all of that just before this, and that chases the fear off.

Frightening? No.

Frighteningly delicious? Absolutely.

I jog a while again, the fact that I crossed that trail renewing my confidence some that I'm making progress. I think part of me feared I was just running in place or something, that I would somehow never get there.

And at some point the sound of distant thunder arises about me. The noise fades in. I'd say that's the most accurate way to put it. It doesn't crash all violently or anything. It's just a constant rumble somewhere far away, swelling and shrinking and turning over onto itself. In some way, the rhythm reminds me of the ocean.

Maybe it's that sound that draws my attention, or maybe it's just running a long way in such a peaceful place, but my mind wanders. My thoughts turn further and further inward until I'm no longer all that conscious of the world outside. My consciousness sucks up into my head, almost all of it.

I try to fit the puzzle pieces of my life together based not on reason but on feeling. It's hard to describe since it comes to me in emotions that are more like colors than words, and maybe it can only make sense inside and not outside.

I think of the white world, and I feel a sense of incomplete things made whole, imperfect beings made perfect. It's almost overwhelming, the feeling it gives me, and somewhere in my belly erupts a twinge of nausea at the sheer intensity of it.

That fades as I think of Glenn, and I feel the sun shining down, the light guiding me, warming me. I see the pink glistening on his Explorer's bumper in my imagination and feel the sense of clarity I felt when we were back in those cells and he gave that long speech about fear and love. And then I see him open the wall and walk through, the light washing over his being to the point of total obscurity.

Those feelings morph when I think of Babinaux, and I feel the Earth itself, the way the soil nurtures the plants, the life it gives, the nourishment. I picture her touching my arm, the way she was moved to the verge of tears by the care she feels for me even though I'm a little shit mouth to her about half of the time. I feel her hugging me, and I feel love. Not romantic love, you know. That is something else all together, much more complicated. What I feel now is the most basic and perhaps most pure love a human being can feel for another, even if they don't know each other all that well. The big love that weaves us all together. The thing that makes someone brave getting hit by a train to pull a stranger off of the tracks. The love that heals us and saves and us and comforts us and makes us want to stick around a while, even with all the pain and death all around us.

I think of Louise, and I feel bliss and fulfillment peppered with pangs of frustration and doubt. It's all mixed up, with strong feelings on both sides. I see her twisting her hair while she reads a book, and then that flashes to that warped reflection of myself I saw in the deprivation tank. This puzzle piece doesn't seem to fit with the others as well somehow. There's a murkiness surrounding it. Trying to make sense of it is like trying to look through clouded water.

And the wet snaps me out of it. My consciousness wakes up to my physical surroundings. The grass smears wet on my feet with every step now, droplets of frigid water that confuse me. I bring my hand to my face to brush at my brow and realize that it's wet as well. In fact, I'm soaked from head to toe.

I stop. I try to remember how this could have happened. How could I get this wet without realizing it? It's definitely not raining.

Wait.

I paw at the air with my hand and tendrils of mist undulate in response and then resettle into motionlessness. Nearly microscopic drops of fluid hang in the air, and when they're not moving, they're almost invisible. They don't fall or flutter or even float. They are completely motionless until I touch them, stuck in midair.

I wait for a second, curious to see if the mist shifts when the air moves, but it never happens. I guess the air doesn't gust on this side of the trail, or maybe that changed at some point while

I was lost in thought.

Looking up, I realize that I'm much closer to the tree now as well. Its immensity grows more impressive as I draw near. It looks like a skyscraper with branches coming out of it. Chunks of root breach the Earth around me to form hills of gnarled tree not far ahead of me.

I run.

Soon, I'm among the root hills, surrounded by them. I change trajectories to avoid some, bobbing and weaving and running faster than ever.

And I stop. The overwhelming feeling of being watched crawls over my flesh, pricking it into goose bumps. I hold my breath. My neck cranes in slow motion, my eyes scanning the horizon.

There.

A haggard figure sits atop one of the chunks of root about 150 feet from me, stick thin with a salt and pepper beard that even at this distance reminds me of a lawn hedge in bad need of a trim. I see that he's looking right at me. We regard each other a moment, and he leans back and slides a navy blue baseball cap on his head.

"Took you long enough, Grobnagger," he calls out.

There's a familiar rasp to the voice that immediately conjures memories of Funyuns and wheat grass and vomiting cats: Glenn.

- 28 -

I run over and watch Glenn clamber down from the root, finding footholds and spots to grip as though he has built up some experience at this. He smiles the whole way down, but his body language betrays his facial expression. His hands and feet know where to go, but when he shifts his weight, I sense hesitation and pain in his demeanor.

Indeed. Upon touching down, he grimaces, the corners of his mouth turning down to expose his clenched teeth.

"Are you OK?" I say.

"It's fine," he says. His eyes glance in the general direction of his feet for a moment, and I note that he's wearing shoes rather than his usual sandals. "I'll explain it all later. Come here."

He hugs me. He smells a bit like a barn, but I'm glad to see him. He's so thin now, he feels almost frail. Coils of beard hair graze my cheek as we part, scraping at me like steel wool.

"I found Amity here," I say. "I didn't get a chance to tell you about it, but we've met up a couple of times in the... wherever we are."

"She told me," he says. He smiles. "Yeah, as soon as she said a naked guy chased her through the desert with a crazy look on his face and his genitals flopping around like a puppy on a trampoline, I was like 'sounds just like Jeff Grobnagger.'"

173

We chuckle, but my mind abandons the humor and races to the next question.

"So you found her?" I say. "Where is she?"

His smile fades.

"We got separated," he says. "Or, well… I got captured, and she managed to get away, I should say."

"Captured? By who?" I say.

"Look, there's really not time to go into all of the details," he says. "Let's get out of here while we can."

After saying this, however, he stops and stares at me, tilting his head back and forth like he's sizing something up.

"Are you high?" he says.

"No," I say. "Well, I mean, in a way, yeah. Aren't you?"

"Not at all," he says.

"Whenever I arrive here, I'm sort of high, and everything looks all white," I say. "I thought it must be like that for everyone."

"That's interesting," he says. "I guess it must be a little different for each of us."

He leads the way toward the tree, but he limps along at a much slower pace than I'm used to. His breathing gets all heavy, and flecks of spit froth between his teeth. I want to ask questions, but his intensity puts me off of it. We walk in the thunder and the hissing and wheezing without a word between us.

The mist sops and soaks and chills me down, especially since we've slowed to this mosey. It saps my body heat away from me one tiny droplet at a time.

The grass grows sparse and gives way to bare dirt as we get even closer to the tree, and the mist seems to cut off as well. My bare feet leave footprints in the soil, which is gray and sandy.

Glenn bends over and puts his hands on his knees. He fights for breath.

"What's wrong?" I say.

"It's nothing," he says. "I'm old. Just give me a minute."

As he leans over, I notice a charm dangling from a chain around his neck. It sort of looks like a hand, palm open, fingers pointed down.

"What's with the necklace?" I say.

"It's for protection," he says, tucking it back into his shirt. "Not that it has done me much good."

I want to ask protection from what, but he launches into a coughing fit. His face turns all red and veins bulge every which way from his forehead and throat. He spits a few times.

I don't think he has a cold or anything like that. I think old people just hack up crazy gobs of stuff periodically. Like my grandfather? He used to just spit phlegm into the garbage all the time. All day, every day. Insane. No particular cause. His old body just produced mucus at a very high rate, especially when he was active. It's like everybody turns into a weird troll when they get old or something. So I will fit right in.

"Let's go," he says all gravelly.

He wipes his chin with the heel of his hand. He looks miserable.

We stride on, kicking up dust in all directions. I look over and see Glenn's eyes narrow to slits. Again, his grimace reveals clenched teeth. I guess he must be in a lot of pain.

I wonder what the hell happened, but I can't bug him now. He can barely breathe, let alone speak.

We walk a long time without saying anything, and the tree

seems to sneak up on me. I look up, and we're there. We're less than 100 feet from it. The girth is inconceivable.

"We need to tread lightly up here," Glenn says through gritted teeth. "Just remember to take it slow and think everything through before we act."

Upon getting this out, he gasps in pain. Again, I have follow up questions that will have to wait.

Up close, I realize there's the faintest red hue to the bark near the base of the trunk. Moving in, divots and crevices pock the outside of the tree, running jagged indentations that form a mess of crooked lines. It's a thick bark with a lot of texture.

We take a few more paces, and Glenn suddenly leans forward and vomits on the ground. And for some reason, for a split second I think maybe the tree is making him sick, being this close to it. But nah, it wouldn't make much sense. I think whatever is paining him is effing him up pretty good.

He holds a hand up to me, I guess preventing me from asking after his condition.

"I'm OK," he says, head still tilted toward the ground.

After a long stretch of heavy breathing, he pulls himself to his feet, and we walk the last few feet to stand by the tree.

So this is it. It strikes me for the first time that there's not really anything to do upon arriving at such a huge tree. If it were a normal tree, we could entertain the possibility of climbing it, though we wouldn't since it'd be pointless. This way, we don't even get the option of considering climbing it before we shut the idea down. We just crane our necks to look up at the monstrous thing.

Pretty big.

"Look," Glenn says.

He points to the ground where I see a shape etched into the sand, and then as we circle the tree, it becomes apparent that there are three such shapes forming a triangle around the base of the trunk. The first shape appears to be a snake like shape forming a sideways figure 8. Next, there's the waves of the ocean, and the last image depicts a flag billowing in the wind.

"What do you see?" he says.

I explain it to him.

"I figured it would be something like that," he says. "We all see something different here. It's showing us something. I think it's like when you chose the cup, remember? I see the sun, a lion and a lightning bolt."

I think about this.

"Do you mean the tree is showing us?" I say.

He doesn't answer. He seems lost in thought, staring into the sand. I kind of think it's not the tree, though.

Still, it's an interesting piece of timber even if it's not communicating with us through sand symbols. I move closer and see little clusters of moss clinging to the bark that make it look like the tree sprouts green five o'clock shadow.

"They're symbols," Glenn says, his voice so hushed I'm not sure if he's talking to me or himself.

"It's a lemniscate," he says.

"What?" I say.

"The shape you described," he says. "It's not a snake forming a sideways figure 8. It's a lemniscate, the infinity symbol. It represents the way that energy cannot be created or destroyed. It stays in motion forever, the way the line of an 8 wraps around and around itself endlessly."

"Oh," I say, but I'm not paying that close of attention. I'm too drawn in by the crazy texture of the tree.

"And the ocean represents mystery and vastness and the infinite possibilities all around us," he says. "It's the force so massive and deep we almost can't understand it. It is something bigger and stronger than us."

I step around the ocean to avoid mussing up the drawing and reach my fingers out to feel the bark.

Glenn gasps, and the last thing I hear before I put my hand on the tree is his voice yelling:

"Grobnagger, wait!"

- 29 -

Before I open my eyes, they come to me, flashes of fire, of blackened skin cracked and peeling, of my body shriveled down to gristle and bone. But it doesn't scare me. It feels like a memory of something that happened a long time ago, immobile and nonthreatening images, like old pictures glued to the pages of a photo album.

I feel no fear. I feel renewed.

I open my eyes and look up through a long stone tube to a circle of illumination above. Something in the nature of the light fills me with certainty that it's morning, I'd guess around 8:30, though maybe my perspective is skewed since I'm trying to judge this from the bottom of a well. Still, even if the precise time is wrong, I believe it to be morning.

I prop myself up on my elbows and examine my body in the paltry light. I'm fine from what I can see, no signs of burns. I run my hands over my skin, calloused fingers scouring abdominals and pectorals and so on. Everything feels normal, smooth, the nerve endings all coo and murmur when I touch them like newborn kittens with their eyes still closed.

I am alive.

I am awake.

I lie back down. The light dims a bit as a cloud passes over the sun, and then, after a beat, the world brightens again. In my mind, I replay my entry into the well. I remember almost falling as I stepped onto the crate, the feel of the rope pressed into my chest, and the lurch and sway of the box teetering under my feet. I smell the chemical stench, the gasoline, all around as I reach the bottom. I see the match tumbling end over end, fluttering down like a toy soldier with a plastic bag parachute dropped down the steps.

But wait. I go back earlier. I picture the meal – the fried chicken, the green beans, the blueberry pie bars. I see the old woman nodding at me, reinforcing my choice of the biscuits, though she wasn't eating any herself. And I try to remember whether or not anyone else was eating them.

Could they have been drugged as part of the ritual? Even if it wasn't the biscuits, was it something else?

I feel around for the buckets. They're still here, and they're empty. They're steel, so it's hard to say whether or not they could have withstood a real fire anyway.

If they drugged me, the fire could have been a hallucination, with Randy like a puppeteer controlling the images in my drugged up brain with the power of suggestion.

I remember reading once that getting someone naked is one of the first steps to effectively brainwashing them. Like when you join the army, the first thing they do is get you naked, give you a physical in a brusque manner and shave your head and stuff, because that rewires your brain in terms of boundaries on the most basic level. The message in that case is that your body belongs to the army now, and it will do what it likes with you. The old order, the personal space you thought you had a right to, is thrown out, and just like that, they've already taken one step toward convincing you that their authority is absolute, and you should be willing to die rather than to disobey an order.

The same is true for many cults, though. They have rituals that involve getting people naked and vulnerable early on. If you rewire somebody on that most basic level, it opens everything else up. It sets a suggestible tone. Their mind becomes a malleable thing that can be bent to the master's will. Even Charles Manson progressed from drugs and orgies to murder.

I try to recall whether or not Stubs or the old timey sisters ate any biscuits. I remember seeing Stubs chewing, but I don't remember what he was eating.

Damn it.

Well, either way, Randy left me down here all night. That has to be significant. He said it'd only be a half an hour. Of course, he also neglected to mention the drugs and fire.

And for the first time, the idea that they aren't coming back seeps into my head. No matter how accurate or not my speculation about drugged food might be, it's at least plausible that they just left me here, right?

Jesus. What if I'm stuck down here?

I stand up, my fingers tracing lines along the mortared creases between the stones. I test my grip on the wall, but there's no chance of that. Climbing can't happen.

I look up into the circle of light. Judging by the way the rope trails off to the side, they left the crate on the ground beside the wall. That removes any possibility of me throwing buckets at the crate to try to shake it down somehow. As ridiculous as that sounds, at least it'd be something to try.

So it'd be pretty ironic to die of thirst inside of a well,

wouldn't it?

Don't panic. Don't panic. We'll have plenty of time to panic later if it gets all the way dark again.

Staring up at the light makes my eyes ache, so I look down to give them a break.

I hear something crash somewhere up there. It's quiet, but it's there. I look up again.

"Hello?" I say.

I wait.

Nothing.

"Help!" I say. "Is someone there?"

Still nothing.

My eyes water from staring into the sunlight, so I rub at them. There's no use yelling, I know. The sound wouldn't carry very far.

But then there's a new sound. The crate crashes into the wall and wobbles, and soon after the rope begins to rotate the pulley. The wooden box descends upon me.

So Randy did come back. I bet I was right about the biscuits.

The crate touches down next to me, and I step in and grip the rope.

"Ready for lift off," I say, projecting my voice up toward the opening.

The rope goes to work again, but the crate jerks and quakes its way up, much slower than my last ride. I suppose lifting me would be quite a bit more difficult than lowering me. It's hardly a concern vs. the prospect of being trapped down here, in any case.

I ascend in that herky jerky fashion, cupping my junk in my

hands, though it would be a lot funnier to shout "Surprise!" and gyrate in a manner to best flop my genitals around when I get pulled into view. I'm a gentleman, however, not unlike Ryan Seacrest, so I cover myself.

As my crate elevator climbs out of the darkness, more and more light surrounds me. Near the top, a bar of actual sunlight slants across my face, and I close my eyes. I feel its warm touch on that thin skin on my eyelids and across the bridge of my nose, and in a way I do feel reborn after all. It's weird how the simplest things bring the greatest perspective. The sun shining on my face makes me feel so lucky to exist at all, to be conscious of the world and spend my days in awe of the wonders all around me.

The crate stops near the top of the well, but it's a touch too low for me to see out there. There's no welcoming party, but I'm not waiting for anyone's permission before I get the hell out of here. I reach up and grab the lip of the wall, pulling myself up. Now, I'm half expecting Randy and Stubs to rush to my aid any second. They do not.

I yank myself up so my chest rests on the corner of the wall, and then I adjust my grip, placing my hands on the opposite corner. As I do this, I realize this is the most vulnerable moment, so I move with great care, pulling myself forward and swiveling the weight of my legs up at the proper second to swing myself over the wall and onto the dry land.

I land on my side. The open air all around me seems to stretch on forever. I roll over onto my back, looking up into a blue sky. The wind blows and goose bumps ripple across the skin on my arms.

Still no one converges on me or says anything, so I sit up. A man lies on the ground near the other side of the well, his face turned away from me. I'm alarmed for a second, until I take note of the beard hair jutting up from the side of the obscured face and the suede sandals adorning his feet.

"Glenn?" I say.

"Yep," he says, turning toward me. It strikes me that his clothes are different than they were in the white world a bit ago. I suppose mine are, too, though.

"You're back," I say. "Back in the real world, I mean."

"In the flesh," he says. "Most of it, anyway."

He sits up, and I follow his gaze to his left foot. It takes a second to process what I'm seeing. The sandal appears to be empty, but no, it's half empty. No toes occupy their proper place. Instead a cauterized stump ends his foot in the middle of the arch.

I gasp.

"What?" he says. "Oh."

He ruffles his mustache with his thumb and index finger.

"It looks worse than it is," he says.

"Really?" I say. "Cause it looks like about half of your foot is gone."

"Well, yeah," he says. "I guess you're right. It looks about as bad as it is."

"How did this happen?" I say.

"We'll discuss it later," he says. "It's too... I don't want to talk about it."

He stands and dusts himself off, careful to put little weight on his left.

"Come on," he says. "We better find you some pants."

- 30 -

We walk through a cornfield, the stalks all papery and knocked over. Glenn seems to have a good sense of where we are, so I follow his lead. He's slow, but considering the foot thing, I can't blame him. We mount a little bump in the field, not a true hill but something like that. Glenn stops to look around.

"Damn," he says.

"What?" I say.

"See that farmhouse up there?" he says.

I look to the house in the distance and nod.

"I was hoping there'd be some clothes on the line," he says.

I see what he means. The rope bounces in the wind, just as naked as I am.

We press forward, trudging over the soil and the busted up corn plants.

I explain everything that's been happening while we walk – about Farber's burned body and the rituals and the stuff with Louise. Glenn listens, but he doesn't say much.

With every step, we inch closer and closer to town. This is good and bad. The only thing I want is to get home, but it's going to be tricky to get around in civilization while straight freeballing like this. Glenn said people would get the wrong idea about us.

We veer off to the right where the field ends, and within a few paces we're in a cul de sac. Leaving the cover of the corn and soy beans behind, I feel quite exposed. The roads and houses nearby only make it worse.

"We had to head right into this subdivision, huh?" I say.

"I'm just keeping us off of the main roads," he says. "I think we can cut through a few yards and get to a wooded area, keep making progress. But at some point we'll need to cross some streets. Some busy ones."

My balls get butterflies in their stomachs at this prospect. We sneak behind houses as we leave the subdivision and get closer to a real street, weaving around swing sets and flower gardens as we stay in a run of backyards to avoid the traffic. This stretches on for a couple of blocks, and we have to hop one fence along the way. It's almost hard to believe that we haven't run into anyone yet.

We round another corner, and I see the woods Glenn spoke of ahead. We have another block to go, but it looks pretty treacherous.

We hustle through the first yard, which, although it's void of humanity, does feature a grill with smoke spilling out of the sides. I picture someone running out to fling hot dogs and hamburgers at us while yelling a lot.

This does not happen.

The second and third yards prove to be free from obstacles, but the fourth yard is the one I meant when I said treacherous. A chain link fence stands between us and the next yard. By itself, this is no problem, of course. It's just that the chain link fence contains a dog. Some kind of pit bull mix that growls deep and long now that we're close.

To go around, we'd have to go out by the street in either direction, which would mean exposing my nudity to the lunch hour rush. But then, none of those people driving by will stop to bite my genitals or face, so I guess I choose that option.

"Let's go around," I say.

"You sure?" Glenn says.

The dog snaps his jaw in the general direction of my nads.

"Yep," I say.

We hustle out around the front of the house, doing a quick yet quiet walking thing that makes me feel like a naked ninja. Judging by the sound, the traffic hit a lull at just the right moment. Almost no cars go by.

Just as we careen around the corner of the house, inches from moving into the clear, the single WOOP of a police siren chirps behind me. I freeze.

"Run!" Glenn says.

I can't run, though.

Because I'm frozen.

Glenn fast walks a few paces, but he can't really run with his half foot, so he gives up.

"Grobnagger?" a voice calls out from behind me.

It's Dennis. Perfect. I turn and get a look at him, sitting in the front seat of his cruiser. His eyebrows are crinkled up, but he's sort of laughing at the same time. Well, at least he'll have a good story to tell for a couple of days.

"Get in," he says.

I call shotgun, but Glenn rides in the front seat anyway since Dennis says it wouldn't look right for an officer of the law to drive around with a naked dude in the front seat. I guess I can respect that.

"Got a call about a naked white male with orange pubic hair running around in the subdivision over here," he says. "I never would have dreamed it'd turn out to be Jeff Grobnagger. Guess I should have, though."

I look down at my pelvic region.

"You think my pubes are orange?" I say.

"Yeah, bro," Dennis says.

"Big time," Glenn says.

Since he was gone for so long, I sort of forgot how everything is "big time" with Glenn. I wonder where he picked that turn of phrase up. Because he should probably consider putting it back as soon as possible.

"I'm gonna go out on a limb here and guess that this…. situation… has something to do with the League of Light," Dennis says. "Would that be accurate?"

"Yep," I say.

I almost expect Glenn to chime in with another big time, but he fails to. I look over, and his hands are cupped over his eyes. After a second he retracts them. He looks pretty exhausted.

Dennis chatters on the CB for a while. And I realize how tired I am as well, once the prospect of this being over soon finally enters my mind. My nudity induced hyperawareness fades a little, and I slink down in my seat. All of the sore in my back wakes up, that faint ache that accompanies relief once you can finally relax. I stretch and rotate my neck back and forth all slow. Every muscle fiber seems to let go a little bit, and my eyes close.

And as I fall into a deeper and deeper relaxation, I realize that I don't care much about any of this cult stuff. I don't care about who killed Farber or stole his body from the morgue. I don't care about Randy's rituals. I barely even care about what is happening to me and why, at least on the most basic level of my being. See, I really only care about one thing, and I need to talk to Louise as soon as I can. Wait. I need to get dressed as soon as I can, and then talk to Louise. Would be difficult to have a serious conversation with my dingus flapping in the breeze.

For a while I stay in that floaty place that comes just before sleep. I hover there, just being, my brain shut off for once. I drift along.

And then a little pang of something builds and builds just outside my conscious thoughts. Some part of my brain sends the rest an urgent message about the outside world that arrives in slow motion, like I can see it coming, I can feel it, but it's not quite there yet, still not there, and then BAM! I'm awake, I'm looking around, mildly panicked.

Oh. We're home.

The car stopping in the driveway somehow woke my brain back up. I guess the disruption of the ride's movement maybe shook me out of my lull.

"Thanks for the ride," I say.

"Not a problem, Magic Mike," Dennis says. "If I hear word about any bachelorette parties coming up, I'll be sure to hand out your card. I'll tell 'em Grobnagger's the best dancer in the biz. He goes full nude, so you will get a little something dangled in your face, and his pubes are the color of fire and Cheetohs."

I don't know what to say, so I say:

"Thanks."

We walk into the house, and Glenn moves straight for the

cupboard. He pulls out the unopened package of Double Stufs, gives me a look.

"I made sure to keep Oreos on hand," I say. "Cause I knew you'd be back eventually."

"Jeff Grobnagger, you are a gentleman," he says, ripping open the package.

See? Remember all of that stuff about me and Seacrest being gentlemen? Confirmed.

- 31 -

Home at last. I shower and get dressed. It feels great to cover my balls with multiple layers of fabric. I think Glenn went straight to bed, and I can understand that, but I'm a little too keyed up to sleep. When your life becomes a non-stop series of symbolic adventures transpiring on other planes of reality, it can sometimes be hard to unwind and get some shut eye. It's almost like I'm so happy to be home that I can't stop reveling in my happiness enough to relax all the way. It will come in time, though. It always does.

I lean back on the couch, my back gone all floppy, my chin aimed at the ceiling. I watch the blades of the ceiling fan go round and round. This isn't so bad, anyway – to feel the tension drain out of my back like I pulled some kind of cork near the bottom.

All this time, I imagined myself calling Louise as soon as I stepped out of the shower onto the heated tiles, but for some reason, now that I'm able, I am hesitant to actually do it. I keep touching my phone in my pocket, running my finger back and forth along the jagged edges of the volume button and the jack where the charger plugs in. Something makes me wait.

The ceiling fan clicks with every rotation of the blades. It reminds me of the clocks in high school. I feel like I spent the bulk of my school days watching the clock, waiting for the time to trickle by. When you're a kid, you have nothing but time. It goes all slow. You just want to throw chunks of it away to be done with the boring bits. The older you get, the more precious it becomes, and the harder it gets to wrangle it. Time picks up speed until it's a blurry object blasting by, and you chase after it and reach out for it over and over, but you can never quite wrap your hands around it. You can never quite catch up. And it only goes faster and faster and faster.

I let my head loll to the right side, and the wind from the fan brushes the side of my face with cool. My eyes droop closed. Everything goes really still, and I realize that I no longer hear the click of the fan. Am I sleeping?

There's a sound, a door opening, footsteps. Is this real or a dream? The click fades back in. It's real.

I jerk myself into an upright position. Louise stands just inside the doorway.

"You're alright!" she says.

She rushes over to me and hugs me, and I feel her warmth against me. She smells clean. I can't think of anything to say right away, so I say nothing.

I lean my head and shoulders back to get a look at her, and to my surprise, she looks pretty sad.

"What's wrong?" I say.

"It's nothing," she says. "Just…"

She trails off into silence. The only thing I can figure is that she was so worried about me that she's still sort of upset. Something like that? I don't know. Trying to figure out how a girl feels is like trying to solve a Rubik's cube in the dark.

"Look, I've been thinking about a lot of stuff that I wanted to talk to you about," I say. "I have this problem accepting affection. My fears get so big, I think that it clouds everything else up, and I can't believe in the good things anymore. And I think I am bad to you and to me sometimes because of it. I injure myself, and it effects how I treat you."

She doesn't say anything. She just looks really sad.

"But it's ok," I say. "Cause I can learn. I can do better. I can be better to you and to myself."

Still nothing.

"What are you thinking about?" I say.

She takes a breath.

"Jeff, I think we want different things," she says.

"What do you mean?" I say.

"Just that you seem quite a bit more serious about all of this than me. About us," she says. "I'm not looking for any kind of commitment or anything like that. I just want to have fun. But you are so sincere and sweet and serious. I just don't think it's right to carry on with you getting the wrong idea."

Her words wash over me in waves. I can only process little bits of it at once, so each wave carries a little more information over the wall of shock and into my brain.

"Oh, yeah," I say. "I get it."

I do the nonchalant shrug.

An awkward pause follows.

"I should go," she says.

"Right," I say.

She walks to the door, slides her shoes on. She yanks open the door.

"It might be weird for a while, but we should stay friends, OK?" she says, standing in the open door.

"Right," I say.

She walks through the doorway into the sunlight and steps away from the building, the door clicking shut behind her.

After she's gone, I do the nonchalant shrug again, like it might convince me it's not so bad.

It doesn't.

So take me away from this place, please, as far as I can go. Elevate me to some other plane, and just erase me from this one. Because I could never figure this one out.

I sit, and I clench my teeth and my fists and my mind. I squeeze and squeeze, and my lips curl and veins pop out of everywhere.

But nothing happens.

I try it again, squeezing, arms shaking, torso quivering.

Please.

Nothing, nothing, nothing.

So the white world left me, too.

I flop my head back onto the back of the couch again and watch the blades of the fan chop at the air. I stare straight at the ceiling, but I can barely sit still. It's here again. There's a violence in me now with no place to go.

I go to the fridge and dig out the six pack of Sam Adams nestled in the back. I carry the half dozen beers and the bottle opener with me back to the couch and pop the first. There's more than one way to disconnect your brain.

- 32 -

After the beer is gone, I poke around the kitchen until I find a half gallon bottle of Jameson Irish whiskey under the sink that's about two thirds full. Not a huge whiskey fan traditionally, but it will do.

Drink up, drink up.

I unscrew the cap and tilt the bottle toward my face, which is harder than it sounds because it's large and heavy. Once my mouth connects to the opening, I dump and chug, long and deep. It burns all the way down, but it feels right somehow. It has to burn like that to change you, to take you away from yourself for a while. It has to sting a little so you know it's in there.

I stop and take a deep breath and wipe the moisture from my lips with the back of my hand. My breath feels all heavy with booze fumes and warm. Water fills my eyes, saliva juices up my mouth, and the burn keeps running up and down my throat.

It's not bad, though. Not bad at all. Maybe I could like whiskey after all. Jameson knows what's up.

See, the big nothing has wormed its way inside my brain again, but if I drink enough, I can keep it at bay. I can stave off the emptiness and the loneliness and the hurt and the boredom and the death all around me. I can forget all of that for a while.

195

If you drink enough, the part of your brain that records memory stops functioning. For a while in there, you're running around, talking to people, doing whatever, but the part of your brain that is supposed to remember it all is passed out in the corner. The next morning you wake up with no memories of the prior evening. Chunks of your time are lost forever. It feels like they're erased, but they're not really because they were never there in the first place. People call it blacking out, but I like to think of it as traveling in time. I drink, and the next thing I know, it's 14 hours later, and I'm somewhere else.

Not that I think that will happen to me right now. I mean, I guess it could, but I was just thinking about it.

I take another long guzzle, and I look out the window at the sun shining on the trees and the sidewalk and the street, and it feels weird that it's the middle of the day somehow. I should be looking out there at a blackened sky. It should be the night time, so late that I'm the only one left awake.

And my phone gurgles. It's a text from Babinaux. It's just a question mark.

"Hi," I write.

"Where are you?" she writes.

"At Glenn's," I say.

"I'll be there in twenty," she says.

It's weird. Knowing that someone will be here soon only makes me want to drink more. I take another toot off the big bottle, but I don't go balls out this time. I need to pace myself.

By the time Babinaux arrives, the whiskey has kicked in. I'm pretty effed up. It's too bad, too, because I'm really in the mood to operate some heavy machinery for the first time in a long while.

She knocks at the door. I'm a little too wobbly to answer it, so I just yell:

"Come in!"

Pretty classy.

She enters and crosses the room, her eyes squinted and brow furrowed as she regards me.

"Are you drunk?" she says.

"Yep," I say.

"It's three in the afternoon," she says.

"It feels like the night, though," I say.

When I close my eyes, I can even see the moon hanging low in a sky gone black.

"Is there some occasion that led to this?" she says, pointing at the whiskey bottle on the coffee table.

"Well, no," I say. "I mean, Glenn is back, and Louise dumped me. So it's a sad-abration."

The sympathetic look she sometimes gets crosses her eyes, and now I feel bad that she feels bad.

"Are you OK?" she says.

"Yeah, I guess so," I say.

"What happened?" she says.

"I tried to tell her about that stuff we talked about," I say. "About how I bottle things up and let the negativity get to me. And then she said that I'm too serious and she just wants to have fun. Well, I mean, that was a terrible summary of it, but I guess it's something like that, yeah."

She leans forward and puts her hand on my shoulder.

"I'm sorry," she says.

And I get this weird feeling. Because she didn't try to tell me it doesn't really matter. She didn't try to tell me I'm better off. She didn't try to tell me that what I feel doesn't really matter and I should forget it. Isn't that what people usually do? Try to rationalize some reason that you should just stop being sad. "There are other fish in the sea." "I never really liked her that much, anyway." So on. So forth. What they're really saying is "how you feel doesn't matter, because (insert reason here)."

But something about that pure empathy overwhelms me, and I feel all shaky and tingly around the sternum. And I get up, and I go to the bathroom. And I think I'm about to cry and possibly vomit at the same time. But I don't. And I think that's for the better. Because grown men aren't supposed to cry. Crying after you drink whiskey is punishable by law in Texas, I think. You hand in your man card and are asked kindly to leave the state.

And when I walk out, she's standing in the hall, and she hugs me. And I feel love, like a mother's love, and it's OK. And I think that even if things are all screwed up for me, some of them broken so bad maybe they'll never be right, there are people that care about me, and I am lucky.

We sit in the living room again after that, and I can hear Glenn snoring in the distance.

"So where were you?" she says. "I tried to call a bunch of times."

"I did the ritual in the well, and we got back here this morning," I say. "I left my phone here, and it died, so I didn't know you tried to call."

"Jeff, that was three days ago," she says.

"What?" I say.

"The ritual?" she says. "That was three nights ago."

My brain is too slow to keep up with all of these damn revelations, so the concept of what she's saying washes over me in those slow waves again. I run over every word a few times before I can make the whole idea stick to my cerebral cortex.

"Randy said you took off or something after," she says. "Everybody was kind of freaked out."

I'm speechless. I drool a little bit on myself. Not sure if I can chalk that up to the shock or the whiskey.

Babinaux's phone rings in her purse.

"Here's Randy now," she says.

She takes the call, and I want to listen to her side of the conversation, but I can't. I can only think about the idea that three days have gone by. I guess Glenn said time works differently in the white world. Could that explain it?

"We have to go," she says, interrupting my thoughts. She stands, still looking at the phone like it might change its mind. "Randy called a meeting at the church. He said he knows what happened to Farber's body."

Interesting.

We burst into motion, and everything seems a little hectic. I catch my reflection in the mirror, my hair all smashed weird in some places and poking up in others. I find a dark green winter hat in a basket by the door and pull it on. Maybe it'll even help me avoid some of the freak show type stares I sometimes get around these cult people.

As Babinaux freshens up in the bathroom, I look in on a sleeping Glenn, laid out on his back, snoring like a hibernating bear. I decide not to wake him, and we head off without him.

- 33 -

The church crawls with people. Watching the human figures cluster and march back and forth between each other reminds me of ants swarming and separating in an ant farm, carrying bits of cricket back to the queen. All of this stands in glaring contrast to the emptiness I've encountered upon arriving here the last couple of times. Bodies jitter and pace and fidget and generally struggle to keep still all around me.

Nervous energy permeates the air. Even in my drunken state, I can feel the anxiety like smoke getting in my eyes.

Babinaux and I file in, picking our way through the crowd to take a seat in the second to last row of pews. The hat seems to serve its secondary function well. No one notices me, from what I can see. I suppose the general level of stimulation in the room helps my cause, of course.

The chatter builds. It sounds like a school cafeteria, the drone of a few hundred voices melding into one noise.

A hush spreads among us as Randy steps into the room, sliding open this weird plastic curtain that sets off the side chamber that I believe I heard someone refer to as the study room. Right away it strikes me as odd that he's sporting a baseball cap. I guess maybe he got so caught up in all of this fervor, he forgot he's wearing it, but it seems quite out of place. He slides the divider shut behind him and strides to the pulpit.

"A new dawn rises," Randy says, his voice reaching yet again for those Gandalf tones. "A new era is upon us."

He pauses, and the silence is shocking after the chatter held sway over the room for so long.

"To live and die is the gift we're given, to walk the Earth for a while, and then to pass on," he says. "For some of us, the living lasts a long time, for others, just a short while. Whatever the circumstances, it is a noble thing, to live and to die."

Another pause. An old lady clears her throat somewhere to my left.

"But to live and die and live again?" he says. "That would be beyond human. That would be divine. But search your feelings. Does not some part of you already believe in this? Does not some part of you wonder that your dead loved ones might return? That your dead pets might come home one day? Isn't some part of you just waiting to hear that death isn't certain, isn't necessary? Hasn't it always been waiting for that?"

And then gasps erupt all around, and I'm confused. My eyes dart from side to side, and then I find it. Riston Farber walks through the opened curtain. He's not some shriveled zombie. He's not scarred and blackened. He's not burned at all. He does look very thin, though, and his posture looks worse than when I last saw him.

Following behind him, 10 or so of his minions stream out of the study room. The tops of their heads are shaved like Friars.

The crowd stands. I don't think anybody consciously does this. We just stand in spontaneous awe. It almost doesn't seem real, but another part of me reacts just the way Randy suggested – that I knew this was possible all along. Like the wild part of my brain that believes in magic wants to lord it over the rest of me, it told me so from the start.

As Farber arrives at the front of the room, Randy takes off his hat to reveal that he too has the top of his head shaved. Just then, I lock eyes with Randy, and he looks terrified for two seconds before he composes himself. He does not look at me again.

Farber stands before the crowd, soaking up the adulation. It reminds me of the spoon hurling back in the diner. He coughs then, hacking, dry coughs that sound to rattle from deep within. Several people crowd around to aid him, and I realize he's quite a bit more frail than I realized. His cheeks are all sunken, and the skin around his eyes looks almost purple.

A motion catches the corner of my eye, and I see that Cromwell stands off behind Farber. His hand waves until he sees that he has my attention. He points at me, then he scrapes his finger across his neck in a throat slash motion and points his eyes and thumb at the door.

I'm not the best at charades, but I'm able follow this.

"Gotta go," I say to Babinaux.

I shuffle out with my head down. One head snaps around as I pass, and I think someone spotted me and is about to yell and point, but then the guy sneezes, and I realize that explains the jerky motion.

As I walk through the doorway into the clear, images flash in my head. The flames in the well, the fear on Randy's face a moment ago and Babinaux telling me I'd be gone for three days.

And I think maybe I accidentally resurrected.

- AWAKE IN THE DARK -

Want to read what happens to Grobnagger next?
For more information on the Awake in the Dark series,
please visit http://ltvargus.com/awake3

- SPREAD THE WORD -

Thank you for reading! We'd be very grateful if you could take a few minutes to review it on Amazon.

How grateful? Eternally. Even when we are old and dead and have turned into ghosts, we will be thinking fondly of you and your kind words. The most powerful way to bring our books to the attention of other people is through the honest reviews from readers like you.

- COME PARTY WITH US -

We're loners. Rebels. But much to our surprise, the most kickass part of writing has been connecting with our readers. From time to time, we send out newsletters with giveaways, special offers, and juicy details on new releases.

Sign up for our mailing list at:
http://ltvargus.com/mailing-list/

- ABOUT THE AUTHORS -

Tim McBain writes because life is short, and he wants to make something awesome before he dies. Additionally, he likes to move it, move it.

You can connect with Tim on Twitter at @realtimmcbain or via email at tim@timmcbain.com.

L.T. Vargus grew up in Hell, Michigan, which is a lot smaller, quieter, and less fiery than one might imagine. When not click-clacking away at the keyboard, she can be found sewing, fantasizing about food, and rotting her brain in front of the TV.

If you want to wax poetic about pizza or cats, you can contact L.T. (the L is for Lex) at ltvargus9@gmail.com or on Twitter @ltvargus.

TimMcBain.com
LTVargus.com

Made in the USA
Lexington, KY
18 January 2015